AESOP'S FABLES

This edition published by Parragon Books Ltd in 2017
and distributed by

Parragon Inc.
440 Park Avenue South, 13th Floor
New York, NY 10016
www.parragon.com

Stories retold by Catherine Allison, Anne Rooney, and Claire Sipi
Illustrated by Victoria Assenelli, Livia Coloji, Abigail Dela Cruz, Neesha Hudson,
Sean Julian, Xuan Le, Carmen Saldana, Luisa Uribe, and Laura Wood
Cover illustrated by Wednesday Kirwan
Edited by Laura Baker and Becky Du Pontet
Designed by Duck Egg Blue, Ailsa Cullen, and Deborah Vickers
Production by Juliet Fountain

ISBN 978-1-4748-9249-0

Printed in China

AESOP'S FABLES

PaRragon

Bath • New York • Cologne • Melbourne • Delhi
Hong Kong • Shenzhen • Singapore

Contents

The Ant and the Grasshopper

It was summer. The sun was warm, the days were long, and Grasshopper sat on a blade of grass, singing to herself. Birds were flitting above her, bees were buzzing in the flowers around her, and fruit was ripening on the apple trees by the stream. Her wings glittered like jewels in the sun, and she was happy.

On the ground, an ant ran to and fro. He was collecting plump seeds and juicy leaves and carrying them home on his back. Sometimes, the things he collected were even bigger than he was, but somehow, he always managed to carry them home. As soon as one thing was safe in his storeroom, he would run off again. He did this all summer long.

Grasshopper looked down from her blade of grass and saw Ant struggling to carry a particularly large leaf.

"What are you doing, Ant?" she asked. "Watching you running about is making me tired!"

Ant stopped what he was doing and looked up at Grasshopper.

"I'm collecting food and bedding for the winter," he said. "These summer days won't last forever. I want to have enough to eat and a warm place to sleep when the cold weather comes."

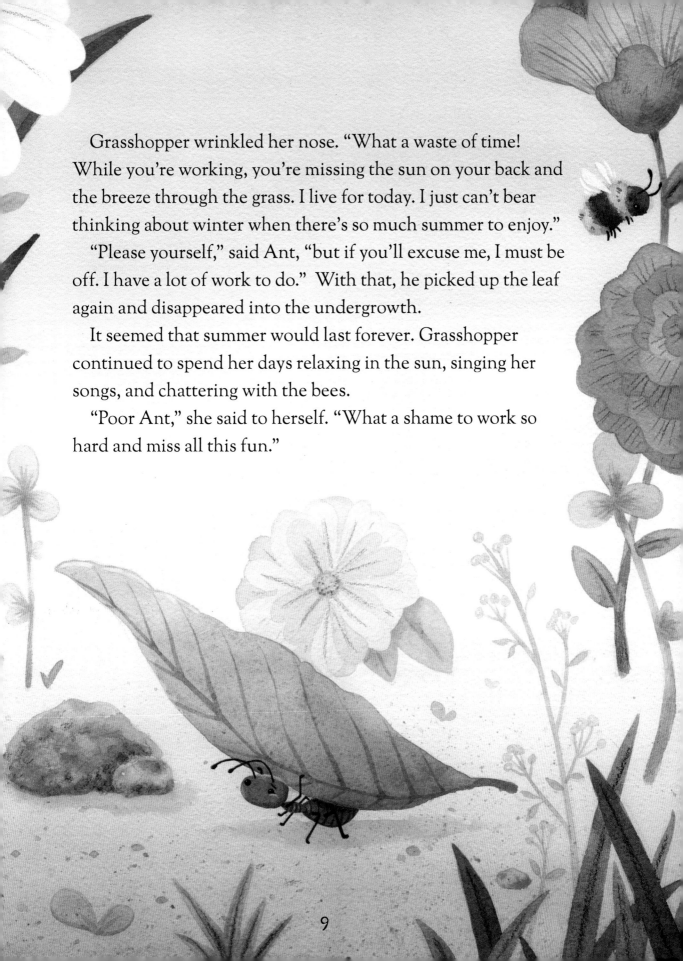

Grasshopper wrinkled her nose. "What a waste of time! While you're working, you're missing the sun on your back and the breeze through the grass. I live for today. I just can't bear thinking about winter when there's so much summer to enjoy."

"Please yourself," said Ant, "but if you'll excuse me, I must be off. I have a lot of work to do." With that, he picked up the leaf again and disappeared into the undergrowth.

It seemed that summer would last forever. Grasshopper continued to spend her days relaxing in the sun, singing her songs, and chattering with the bees.

"Poor Ant," she said to herself. "What a shame to work so hard and miss all this fun."

Then one morning, the weather changed. The sun still shone, but it wasn't warm anymore. The leaves on the apple trees were yellow and a cold wind whirled them through the air. The grass tips were white with frost. The birds flew off to warmer lands, and the bees would not stay and chat with Grasshopper. It was fall.

Grasshopper began to worry that maybe she should be rushing off somewhere, too, but she didn't know where.

Time went by, and fall turned to winter. Now the days were short, and the sun never shone. Frost clung to every stem and stone. The bees had disappeared, and Grasshopper shivered alone on her blade of grass because she had nowhere warm to go.

"I have no food or shelter. How can I survive in the cold?" she whimpered. "I must try to find somewhere out of this wind." She crawled down the grass and buried herself in the leaves on the ground to sleep. The sky grew darker, and the wind howled.

Ant was hurrying home through the undergrowth when he happened to see her half-hidden in the leaves.

"Silly Grasshopper!" Ant thought to himself. "You did nothing but sing and sunbathe all summer, and now look at you." But he was a kind ant, so he took pity on the poor frozen creature.

"Wake up, Grasshopper!" he whispered gently. "You can't stay here any longer in this cold. Let me take you somewhere warm."

Nuts

Seedpods

Currants

Grasshopper opened her eyes, but she was too weak to move, so Ant carried her all the way to his home and then down through tunnels deep in the earth. It was warmer down there, and at last, Grasshopper began to feel better. Looking around to her left and her right, she could see storerooms full of the seeds and leaves that Ant had collected during the summer. Ant had worked very hard indeed, thought Grasshopper miserably.

At last, Ant and Grasshopper reached the end of the tunnel, where there was a large cozy bedroom, with a soft, warm bed.

Grain

Berries

Leaves

"Now, Grasshopper, lie down here and rest," said Ant kindly. "And since you have nowhere else to go and no food, I suppose you had better stay with me this winter."

"Oh, thank you," said Grasshopper, tearfully. "You have saved my life. I was such a fool, wasting all those summer days. I should have been working hard like you, and then I wouldn't be in this trouble. Next year, I'll work all through the summer, I promise."

Moral: Winter will come, so it is best to prepare for it.

The Fox and the Crow

One day, a crow was flying past an open window when she spotted a tasty piece of cheese on the table. There was no one in the room, so she fluttered in and stole it! Then she flew up into the branches of a nearby tree and was just about to eat the cheese, when a fox appeared.

The fox was also particularly fond of cheese, and he was determined to steal the crow's prize.

"Good morning, Mistress Crow," he greeted her. "May I say that you are looking especially beautiful today? Your feathers are so glossy, and your eyes are as bright as sparkling jewels!"

The fox hoped that the crow would reply and drop the cheese, but she didn't even thank him for his compliments. So he tried again: "You have such a graceful neck, and your claws are really magnificent. They look like the claws of an eagle."

Still, the crow ignored him.

The fox could smell the delicious cheese, and it was making his mouth water. He had to find a way to make the crow drop it.

At last, he came up with a plan.

"All in all, you are a most beautiful bird," he said. "In fact, if your voice matched your beauty, I would call you the Queen of Birds. Why don't you sing a song for me?"

Now, the crow liked the idea of being addressed as the Queen of Birds by all the other creatures in the woods. She thought that the fox would be very impressed by her loud voice, so she lifted her head and started to sing.

Of course, as soon as she opened her beak, the piece of cheese fell down, down, down to the ground. The fox grabbed it in a flash and gobbled it up.

"Thank you," he said. "That was all I wanted. I have to say that you may have a loud voice, but you aren't as clever as I am!"

Moral: Be careful around a flatterer.

The Miller, His Son, and the Donkey

Once there was a miller who had a young son and an old gray donkey. The miller was poor, so one day, he decided to sell the donkey. It was old and gray, but it would still fetch a good price at market. The market was in a town a four-hour walk away, so as soon as the sun rose, they set off, the miller striding in front, the donkey trotting beside him, and the miller's son skipping along behind them.

It was a bright sunny morning, and because it was market day, the road was full of people walking to the town or back home. The miller's neighbor was one of them, and he stopped to say hello.

"It's a fine day for a walk, my friend, but why don't one of you ride on your donkey? I've just come back from the market myself, and it's still far from here. Take my advice: You'll all be walking for hours if you don't."

"What a good idea!" said the miller gratefully. "We'll get there much quicker if we do as you say." With that, he helped his son onto the donkey's back, and they set off along the road again, the miller striding in front and his son on the donkey, who was walking behind him.

The road passed between two fields, one of which was full of farmworkers cutting ripe corn. As the miller came along, two of the workers stopped what they were doing and called out, "Your donkey looks strong enough to carry you, Mr. Miller. Why don't you ride on it instead of your son? Take a break, or you will be too tired for the full walk!"

"That's a great idea!" replied the miller happily. "When I've sold the donkey, I'll have no choice but to walk everywhere, but today, I can ride." With that, he took his son's place on the donkey, and they all set off once more, the donkey plodding along, the miller riding, and the miller's son jogging beside them.

After a little while, they came to a broad river, where a group of young women were washing their clothes in the water while their children played in the shade of a willow tree. As the miller passed by, one of them looked up at him and cried, "You should be ashamed of yourself, Mr. Miller! You're riding on the donkey while your little boy has to run to keep up!"

The miller's face turned red with shame. "You're absolutely right," he said. "It was thoughtless of me. After all, there's room on the donkey for both of us. Thank you." The miller lifted up his son to sit in front of him, and they all set off once more, the donkey plodding along slowly with the man and the boy on his back.

They were nearly in the town now, which was just as well, because the donkey was starting to struggle under the weight of the miller and his son. A townsman who was walking past them saw the donkey stumble and frowned at the miller.

"Your donkey is exhausted, poor thing. You and your son should be carrying it, instead of it carrying you!"

"You're absolutely right," said the miller, looking guilty. "I was being thoughtless again. We'll take your advice, sir, and thank you for it."

With that, he and his son jumped off the donkey. They chopped down a tall, slender tree to use as a pole and tied the donkey to it by its hooves. Then they hoisted the pole onto their shoulders and carried the donkey into the market place.

When the stall owners saw them, they fell over laughing.

"Just look at that!" cried one woman, tears of laughter rolling down her cheeks. "That donkey must be very special to be carried to market on a pole. Be careful that you don't let its hooves touch the dirty ground, Mr. Miller!"

The miller felt very silly indeed. He felt even sillier a minute later: The donkey, who was tired of walking and tired of being jiggled along on the pole, kicked out with all four legs together, snapped the ropes that held it to the pole, and fell to the ground. Then it ran off back down the road and into the open countryside, free at last.

The miller and his son stood there, open-mouthed, and watched it disappear. All they could do now was go back home, with no money, no donkey, and very red faces.

Moral: If you try to please everyone, you will please no one at all.

The Birds, the Beast, and the Bat

Along time ago, the birds and the beasts had many disagreements. They decided to have a battle to settle their differences once and for all.

Poor Bat, who had wings like the birds and fur like the beasts, didn't know what to do. He didn't want to fight, but he didn't want to be on the losing side either.

So when the birds asked him who he favored, he quickly replied, "I have wings! I am on your side, of course."

And when the beasts asked him which side he would join, he responded, "Isn't it obvious? I have fur and sharp teeth. I'm with you!"

Luckily, at the last minute, the birds and the beasts made peace, and no battle was fought.

With a huge sigh of relief, Bat went to join in the celebrations. But when the birds and the beasts realized that Bat had been on both sides, they turned on him angrily.

Now, poor Bat lives in fear, hiding in dark places and only flying out at night.

Moral: If you deceive, you will end up with no friends.

The Owl and the Grasshopper

In a dark forest, there lived an owl. She had become very grumpy in her old age and didn't like being woken up from her daily nap.

One afternoon, as the owl dozed in her hollow, a grasshopper began his raspy song.

The owl woke with a start. Poking her head out of the tree, she hooted, "Have you no manners? Go away, and leave me in peace to sleep!"

"You can't tell me what to do!" replied the bold grasshopper. And he began a louder, scratchier tune.

The owl realized she couldn't make the grasshopper stop. So she called out in a sweet voice, "If I must stay awake, come and sing closer to me in my cozy tree."

Flattered, the foolish grasshopper jumped into the owl's dark hollow. The owl tried to stop him from singing by eating him up! Luckily, the grasshopper escaped, but from that day on, he always thought of others before he sang.

Moral: Flattery can sometimes be used for trickery.

The Old Woman and the Fat Hen

There was once an old woman who kept a hen that laid one egg every morning without fail. The eggs were large and delicious, and the old woman was able to sell them for a very good price at market.

"If my hen would lay two eggs every day," she said to herself, "I would be able to earn twice as much money!"

So, every evening, the old woman fed the hen twice as much food.

Each day the old woman went to the henhouse expecting to find two eggs, but there was still only one—and the hen was getting fatter and fatter.

One morning, the woman looked in the nest box, and there were no eggs at all. There were none the next day, nor any the day after that. All the extra food had made the hen so fat and contented, that she had become lazy and had given up laying eggs altogether!

Moral: Things don't always work out as planned.

The Bell and the Cat

Once there was a large family of mice who lived in a big old house. Their lives would have been perfect, except for one thing: There was a cat who lived there, too. Each time the mice crept into the kitchen to nibble a few crumbs, the cat would pounce and chase them until they disappeared under the floorboards.

"If we don't come up with a plan soon, we'll starve," cried Grandfather Mouse.

But the mice couldn't agree on a single idea. Finally, the youngest mouse had a brainstorm.

"We could put a bell on the cat's collar, so that we can hear him coming," he suggested.

All the mice thought this was an excellent plan.

Then Grandfather Mouse stood up. "You are a very smart young fellow to come up with such an idea," he said. "But, tell me, who is going to be brave enough to put the bell on the cat's collar?"

Moral: Coming up with a plan can be easier than carrying it out.

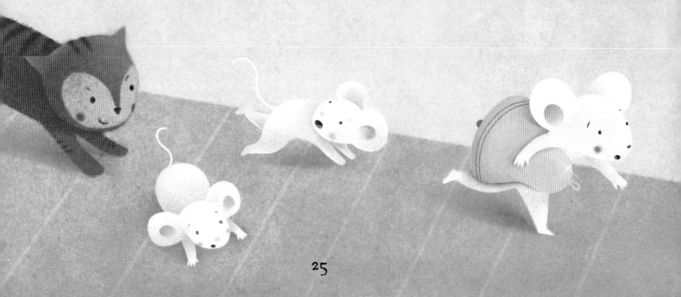

The Vain Crow

Once upon a time, Crow was flying over the gardens of the King's palace, when he spotted a flock of royal peacocks proudly displaying their bright-colored tail feathers. He had never seen such beautiful feathers before, and he was filled with envy.

Crow's own feathers were dull and black. Every time he caught sight of his reflection, he felt unhappy.

"Oh, I wish I had shimmering feathers like the peacocks!" Crow sighed.

One day, Crow found several peacock feathers lying on the ground. They must have fallen from the peacocks' tails. Quickly, he collected them all and stuck them to his own black tail.

"Look at me!" Crow cried proudly, as he strutted up and down in front of the other crows. But the other crows just laughed at him and told him he looked funny.

"I'm going to join the peacocks," Crow cried. "I'm sure they'll be impressed!"

But when the peacocks saw Crow, they laughed, too.

"You're not one of us!" they called. "Go away!" And they plucked out all the peacock feathers he had borrowed.

Poor Crow! Feeling very silly, he flew home. But when the other crows saw him, they scolded him and told him to go away.

Crow realized too late that he should have been happy with who he was, rather than pretend to be something he wasn't.

Moral: It is much better to be yourself than someone you are not.

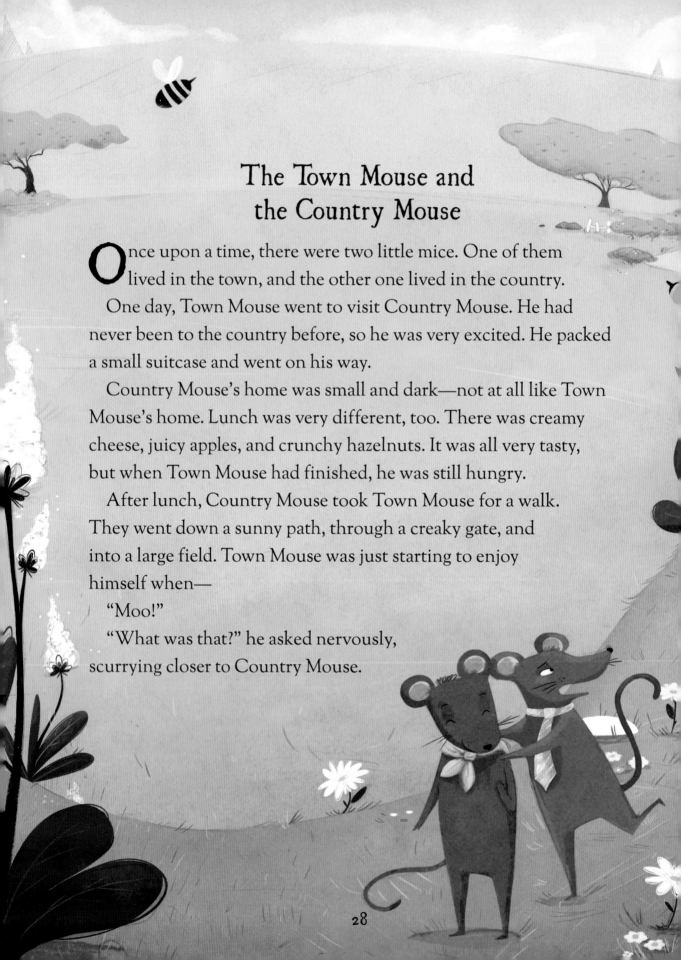

The Town Mouse and
the Country Mouse

Once upon a time, there were two little mice. One of them lived in the town, and the other one lived in the country.

One day, Town Mouse went to visit Country Mouse. He had never been to the country before, so he was very excited. He packed a small suitcase and went on his way.

Country Mouse's home was small and dark—not at all like Town Mouse's home. Lunch was very different, too. There was creamy cheese, juicy apples, and crunchy hazelnuts. It was all very tasty, but when Town Mouse had finished, he was still hungry.

After lunch, Country Mouse took Town Mouse for a walk. They went down a sunny path, through a creaky gate, and into a large field. Town Mouse was just starting to enjoy himself when—

"Moo!"

"What was that?" he asked nervously, scurrying closer to Country Mouse.

"Ha! That's just a cow," said his friend. "There are lots of them in the country. It's nothing to be scared of."

Town Mouse and Country Mouse strolled on, through a flowery meadow and over a grassy hill. Soon, they came to a peaceful pond. Town Mouse was just starting to enjoy himself when—

"Hiss!"

"What was that?" he asked again, quivering from nose to tail.

"Ha! That's just a goose," said his friend. "There are lots of them in the country. It's nothing to be scared of."

Town Mouse and Country Mouse continued walking, across a rickety bridge, down a sandy track, and into a shady wood. Town Mouse was just starting to enjoy himself when—

"Twit-twoo!"

"What was THAT?" he yelped, and he jumped off the ground in terror.

"It's an owl!" cried Country Mouse. "Run for your life! If it catches you, it will eat you up!"

So the two mice ran and ran until they found a leafy hedge to hide in.

Town Mouse was terrified. "I don't like the country at all!" he said. "Come to stay with me in the town. You'll see how much better it is!"

Country Mouse had never been to the town before, so he packed a small backpack and went to stay with his friend.

Town Mouse's home was huge and grand, not at all like Country Mouse's home.

Lunch was very different, too. Instead of apples and nuts, there was cake and ice cream and chocolates. Lots and lots of them. It was tasty, but soon, Country Mouse began to feel a bit sick.

After dinner, the friends went out for a walk. They walked past shops and offices and houses. Country Mouse was just starting to enjoy himself when—

"Beep-beep!"

"What's that?" he asked fearfully, looking around him.

"That? It's just a car," said his friend. "There are lots of them in the town. It's nothing to be afraid of."

Then the mice walked through a park, past a church, and down a wide road. Country Mouse was just starting to enjoy himself when—

"Nee-nah! Nee-nah!"

"What's that?" he asked again, his whiskers twitching.

"That's just a fire engine. There are lots of them in the town. It's nothing to be afraid of."

As the mice pitter-pattered home, they passed a playground, a school, and a pretty garden. Country Mouse was just starting to enjoy himself when—

"Meow!"

"What's that?" he squeaked, his eyes as wide as saucers.

"It's a cat!" cried Town Mouse. "Run for your life! If it catches you, it will eat you up!"

So the two mice ran and ran, all the way back to Town Mouse's home.

Country Mouse was terrified. "I don't like the town at all! I'm going home," he said.

"But how can you be happy living near the cow and the goose and that horrible owl?" said Town Mouse.

"They don't scare me!" cried Country Mouse. "How can you be happy living near the cars and the fire engines and that terrible cat?"

"They don't scare me!" cried Town Mouse.

The two mice looked at each other. Who was right and who was wrong? They would simply never agree. So they shook hands and went their separate ways, Town Mouse to his grand home and Country Mouse to his cozy one.

"Home sweet home!" said Town Mouse, sighing a deep, happy sigh.

"Home sweet home!" said Country Mouse, smiling a big, happy smile.

And the two of them lived happily ever after, each in their own way.

Moral: Be grateful for what you have, because what someone else has is not always best for you.

The Fox and the Tree

One day, a bold young fox was trotting along feeling very happy with himself: For breakfast, he had gobbled up a plump hen, right under the farmer's nose, then for lunch, he had found two large rabbits—they had never even heard him coming! He was such a clever fox!

All of a sudden, the most delicious smell wafted through the air and tickled his nose. It smelled like hot toast with melting cheese, apple pie and custard, and beef stew with dumplings, all rolled into one. Even though he wasn't really hungry, the fox licked his lips.

"If it tastes even half as good as it smells," he said to himself, "it must be the most delicious food in the world. Where can that smell be coming from?"

Another wave of deliciousness wafted through the air, and he followed it to a large old oak tree, standing on its own in a field. The smell seemed to be coming out of a small hollow in the trunk.

"There must be food hidden inside," thought the fox. "Perhaps the farmer has left his lunch here while he's working in a nearby field. He thought the hollow was so small that his food would be safe, but he was wrong. I'm going to steal it!"

The fox looked into the hollow. The hollow was small, but it led to a large space inside the tree, and in the middle of that space was indeed the farmer's lunch. There was a fresh sandwich with lots of ketchup, and a warm pie, with golden, crumbly pastry on top. The fox jumped for joy.

Still, how was the fox going to get to the food? He reached one long paw through the hole, but he couldn't even touch it. No matter how much he stretched, he could not reach the delicious food.

"If my paw isn't long enough, I'll just have to squeeze inside myself," he said.

So he squeezed and wriggled himself through the hole into the hollow tree. Once inside, he gobbled up all the food. It tasted twice as good as it had smelled! When he had finished, he lay back and patted his bulging tummy happily. He was REALLY full.

The fox must have dozed off because when he woke, it was dark inside the tree. "I must go home," he thought, so he struggled to his feet and stretched his front paws out through the hole. Then he pushed his head and shoulders through and tried to squeeze the rest of his body after them. He wriggled and he stretched, but he couldn't get his bulging tummy through. It was much too big. He was stuck.

"Oh no!" said the fox. "What am I going to do?"

It was completely dark now, and the fox felt very uncomfortable, half inside and half outside the tree. He started to whimper and whine, hoping that someone nearby would come and help him to get free.

A small brown rabbit happened to be passing by the tree, and she heard the fox's whimpering. Normally, she was scared of foxes and wouldn't get too close, but when she saw that he was trapped, she hopped up to take a look.

"Why are you in that hole, Fox?" she asked politely. "You look very funny."

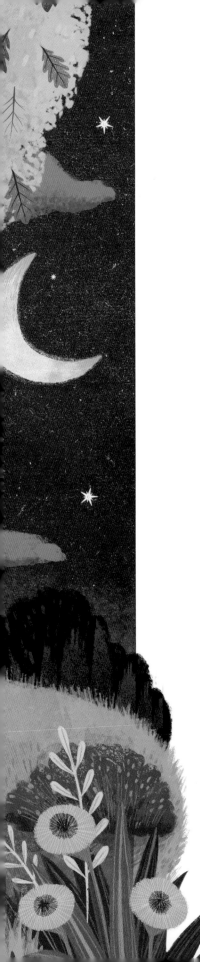

"Oh, Rabbit, dear Rabbit!" whimpered the fox. "Please help me. I smelled a delicious smell coming from inside this tree, so I just climbed in to take a look, and now I can't get out. The hole must have gotten smaller while I was inside."

The rabbit looked hard at the fox. She knew how much he liked to eat, and if he had found delicious food, she was sure he would have eaten it.

"Are you sure that the hole has gotten smaller, or have you gotten bigger?" she said with a smile. "You silly fox, you shouldn't have eaten so much." With that, she turned to go.

"Don't go," cried the fox. "I don't want to stay here all alone. Tell me what I can do to get free?"

"Staying there is all you can do, I'm afraid," said the rabbit. "But don't worry. In a few days, you'll be slim again, and then you can go home. Perhaps spending a few days stuck in this tree will teach you not to be so greedy in the future."

Then the rabbit hopped off across the field, and the fox was left alone, with nothing to do but think about how silly and greedy he had been. Sure enough, a few days later, his tummy was smaller, so he slipped out of the hollow in the trunk and slunk back home.

Moral: It is best not to be greedy.

The Swallow and the Crow

One day, a young swallow landed on a branch next to his friend, the wise old crow. The swallow looked down his beak at the crow and said, "I don't think much of your stiff feathers. You should take better care of how you look."

The old crow was very angry and was about to fly away, when the swallow continued, "Look at me with my soft downy feathers. They are what a well-dressed bird needs."

"Those soft feathers of yours might be all right in the spring and summer," the crow replied. "But in the winter, you have to fly away to warmer countries. In the winter, the trees are covered in ripe berries. I can stay here and enjoy them because I have my stiff black feathers to keep me warm and dry."

The crow held out his wings. "What use are your fancy feathers then, Swallow?" he asked, before turning away.

Moral: Fair-weather friends are not worth much.

The Dog and His Reflection

A hungry dog passed a butcher shop and spotted a juicy steak lying on the counter. He waited until the butcher went to the back of the shop, then he ran in and stole it.

On his way home, the dog crossed a narrow bridge over a river. As he looked down into the water, he saw another dog looking up at him. This dog was also carrying a piece of meat, and it looked even bigger than the one he had!

"I want that steak, too," thought the greedy dog. So he jumped into the river to steal the steak from the other dog.

But as he opened his mouth to snatch the steak, the butcher's steak fell from his mouth and sank to the bottom of the river. The other dog vanished in a pool of ripples.

The greedy dog had been fooled by his own reflection, and now he was still hungry and had nothing left to eat!

Moral: Being greedy can leave you with nothing at all.

The Boy Who Cried Wolf

Once upon a time, there was a boy named Peter who lived in a little village in the mountains with his parents, who were sheep farmers. It was Peter's job to watch over the flock and protect the sheep from wolves.

Day after day, Peter sat on the mountainside watching the flock. It was very quiet with no one but sheep for company. No wolves ever came to eat the sheep.

Peter got very bored. He tried to amuse himself by climbing rocks and trees or by crawling through the grass and counting the sheep, one by one.

"One, two, three ... sixty-four, sixty-five ..." counted Peter. "Oh, I wish something exciting would happen. I'm so BORED! Same old mountain, same old sheep ..."

Finally, one day, Peter couldn't stand being bored anymore.

"I know what to do!" he grinned to himself.

He scrambled up a nearby tree and started shouting at the top of his voice,

"WOLF! Help! WOLF!"

42

Down in the village, a man heard Peter's cries.

"Quick!" he shouted to some other men. "We need to help Peter. There's a big wolf attacking the sheep."

The villagers grabbed their axes, forks, shovels, and brooms and ran up the mountain to where Peter was shepherding his flock.

When they got there, puffing and panting, all was quiet, and the sheep were grazing peacefully.

"Where's the wolf?" one of the villagers cried.

Still sitting in the branches of the tree, Peter roared with laughter. "There's no wolf. I was just playing!"

The men were very angry with Peter. "You mustn't cry wolf when there isn't one," they said.

That night, Peter was scolded by his mother and was sent to bed without any supper.

For a while after this, Peter managed to behave himself. He climbed the mountainside with the sheep every day and watched over them quietly. The villagers soon forgot about his trick.

Then one day, Peter got really bored again. He had already run up and down the rocks, climbed three trees, and counted the sheep ten times.

"What can I do now? Same old mountain, same old sheep ..." he groaned to himself.

With a sigh, he slumped to the ground. As he was sitting there, an idea popped into his head. He picked up some sticks lying nearby and started banging them hard together. Then, at the top of his voice, he shouted, "WOLF! Help! WOLF! Please hurry, there's a big wolf eating the sheep!"

Down in the village, a crowd of people started gathering when they heard the loud banging and shouting coming from the mountainside.

"What's all that noise?" someone cried.

"It's Peter. He's in trouble!" shouted someone else. "Quick, there must be a wolf on the prowl."

Once again, the men grabbed their axes, forks, shovels, and brooms. They ran up the mountain to chase away the wolf and save poor Peter and his sheep.

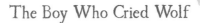

And once again, when they got there, puffing and out of breath, all was quiet, and the sheep were grazing peacefully.

"Peter, what's happened?" shouted one man angrily.

"There's no wolf," laughed Peter. "I was only playing."

"You shouldn't make jokes like that," said another man. "It's not good to lie." The men marched back down the mountain toward the village.

That night, Peter got an even bigger scolding from his mother and once again had to go to bed without any supper.

For a few days, the villagers went around moaning about Peter and his tricks. But after a while, the incident was forgotten, and Peter continued to climb the mountainside every day with the sheep.

He decided that he would try to behave himself, especially since he didn't want another scolding from his mother.

A few weeks later, while Peter stood counting the sheep as usual to pass the time, he noticed that some of them were bleating nervously. He climbed up a tree to take a look around and see what was upsetting them.

To his horror, he saw a big, hairy wolf. The terrifying creature was creeping through the grass toward the flock with its jaws open and its long tongue hanging out. Peter could see the wolf's sharp, pointed teeth.

Shaking with fear, he started screaming, "WOLF! Help! WOLF! Please hurry, there's a big wolf about to eat the sheep!"

A few people down in the village heard his cries for help, but they continued with their business as usual. "It's only Peter playing another trick," they said to each other. "Does he think he can fool us again?"

And so nobody went to Peter's rescue.

By nightfall, when Peter hadn't returned, his parents became concerned. Peter never missed his supper—something bad must have happened.

Peter's father quickly gathered the men of the village, and together, they hurried up the mountain, carrying flaming torches.

Peter was still in the tree when the men found him, shaking and crying. All the sheep had run away.

"I cried out wolf! Why didn't you come?" he wept.

"Nobody believes a liar, even when he's speaking the truth," said Peter's father, helping him climb out of the tree. Peter hung on to his father all the way home. He never wanted to see another wolf ever again.

And Peter finally really learned his lesson. He never told lies again, and he always got to eat his supper.

Moral: Do not tell lies, because no one will believe you when you tell the truth.

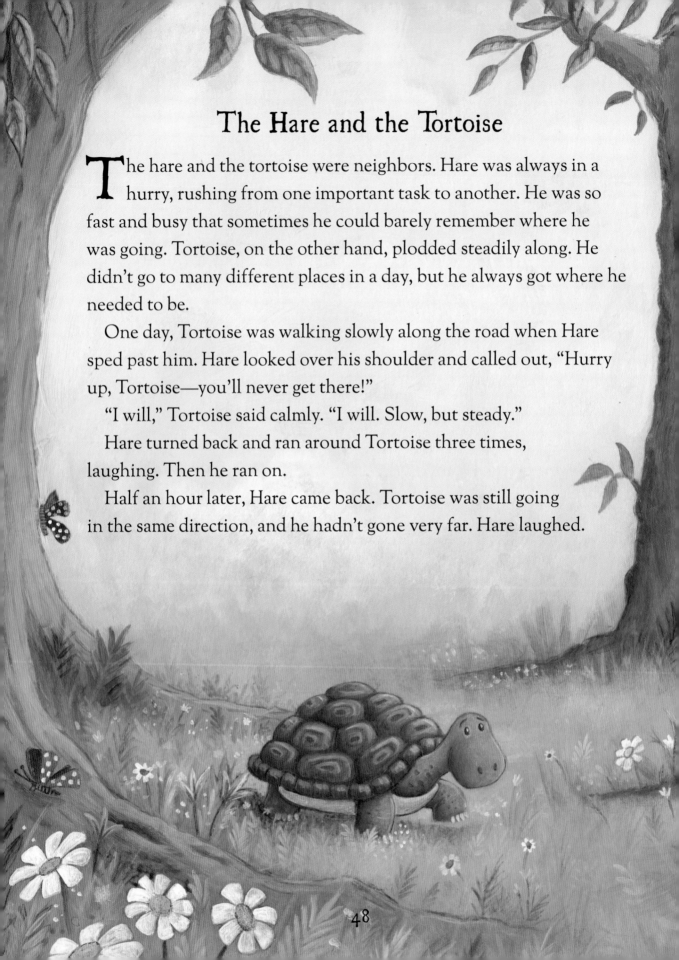

The Hare and the Tortoise

The hare and the tortoise were neighbors. Hare was always in a hurry, rushing from one important task to another. He was so fast and busy that sometimes he could barely remember where he was going. Tortoise, on the other hand, plodded steadily along. He didn't go to many different places in a day, but he always got where he needed to be.

One day, Tortoise was walking slowly along the road when Hare sped past him. Hare looked over his shoulder and called out, "Hurry up, Tortoise—you'll never get there!"

"I will," Tortoise said calmly. "I will. Slow, but steady."

Hare turned back and ran around Tortoise three times, laughing. Then he ran on.

Half an hour later, Hare came back. Tortoise was still going in the same direction, and he hadn't gone very far. Hare laughed.

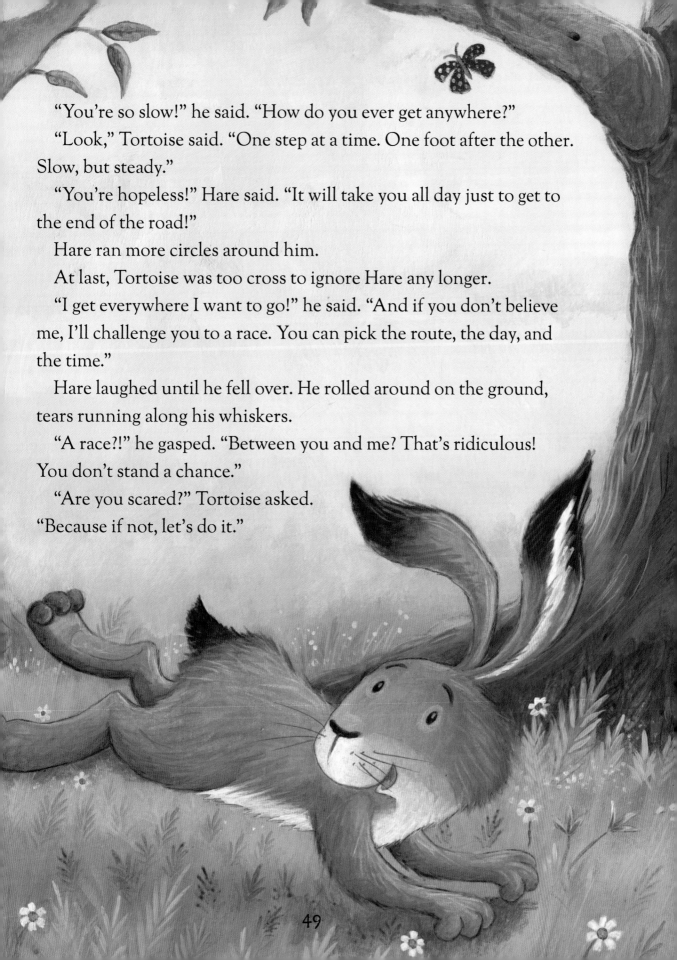

"You're so slow!" he said. "How do you ever get anywhere?"

"Look," Tortoise said. "One step at a time. One foot after the other. Slow, but steady."

"You're hopeless!" Hare said. "It will take you all day just to get to the end of the road!"

Hare ran more circles around him.

At last, Tortoise was too cross to ignore Hare any longer.

"I get everywhere I want to go!" he said. "And if you don't believe me, I'll challenge you to a race. You can pick the route, the day, and the time."

Hare laughed until he fell over. He rolled around on the ground, tears running along his whiskers.

"A race?!" he gasped. "Between you and me? That's ridiculous! You don't stand a chance."

"Are you scared?" Tortoise asked. "Because if not, let's do it."

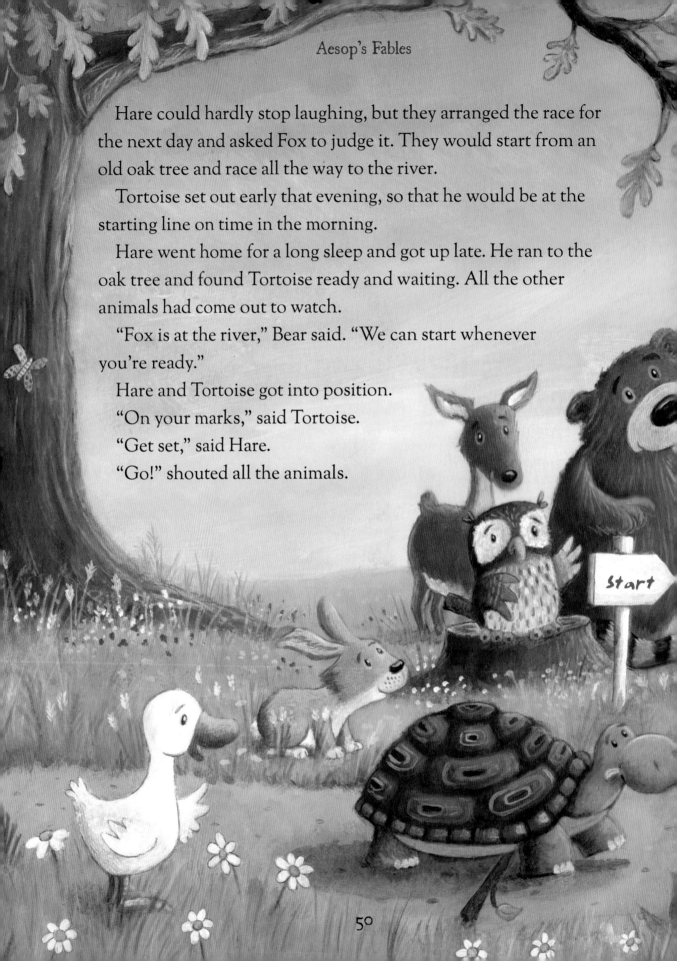

Hare could hardly stop laughing, but they arranged the race for the next day and asked Fox to judge it. They would start from an old oak tree and race all the way to the river.

Tortoise set out early that evening, so that he would be at the starting line on time in the morning.

Hare went home for a long sleep and got up late. He ran to the oak tree and found Tortoise ready and waiting. All the other animals had come out to watch.

"Fox is at the river," Bear said. "We can start whenever you're ready."

Hare and Tortoise got into position.

"On your marks," said Tortoise.

"Get set," said Hare.

"Go!" shouted all the animals.

Start

And off went the tortoise and the hare.

Hare sprinted ahead, bounding through the grass with his tail bobbing up and down. Tortoise lifted one foot and put it down. Then he lifted the other foot and put it down. Slowly, slowly. By the time he reached the first bush, Hare was a tiny spot in the distance. By the time he reached the second bush, Hare was nowhere to be seen.

After a few minutes, Hare could see the river ahead. He paused and looked around. He couldn't see Tortoise at all.

"He is so slow!" he laughed to himself. "He won't be here for hours. I might as well rest for a while." So Hare sat down under a tree. The sun was warm, and the lazy buzz of bees visiting the flowers around him was soothing. Soon, Hare dozed off.

Back in the grass, Tortoise kept going, slow but steady, one step at a time, one foot after the other.

After an hour, Hare woke up and peered into the distance. He could just see Tortoise coming toward him, slow but steady, and still far away.

"He's so slow!" Hare said to himself. "He won't be here for hours. I might as well go back to sleep." And that's just what he did.

Tortoise continued, slow but steady, his heavy shell wobbling along the path. Hare slept on in the hot sun.

When Hare woke up, he couldn't see Tortoise anywhere.

"Where has he gone?" he said. "He won't be here for hours, I'm sure. I could just go back to sleep." But it was late afternoon, and the sun was low in the sky.

"I'm sick of this race," Hare said to himself. "I should finish, so I can go nap in my own bed." And he sprang up and ran as fast as he could to the finish line.

Tortoise was waiting for him by the river.

"Where have you been?" asked Tortoise. "I've been here for hours. You are so slow!"

Hare tried to explain, but neither Tortoise nor Fox would listen.

"But I'm faster!" Hare complained. "It's not fair!"

"The rules were simple," Fox said. "Tortoise won."

"The race was to get here first," Tortoise smiled, "not to run fastest." And slowly, steadily, he turned around to begin his journey home.

Moral: Slow and steady wins the race.

The Ant and the Dove

One morning, a thirsty ant went down to the river for a drink. Suddenly ... SWOOSH! A ripple swept the tiny ant off the riverbank and into the water.

"Help!" cried the ant.

A kind dove heard the ant's cries. She swooped down and dropped a leaf into the water near him.

"Climb onto this," she cooed.

"Oh, thank you," gasped the ant. "You saved my life!" He floated back to the shore on the leaf.

A little while later, the ant was drying off in the sun when he saw a hunter trying to catch the dove with a net.

The ant wanted to help his new friend, so he scurried over to the hunter and bit his foot.

"Ouch!" yelled the hunter.

Startled by the noise, the dove flew away.

"Thank you," she called out to the ant. "Now you've saved my life, too!"

Moral: One good turn deserves another.

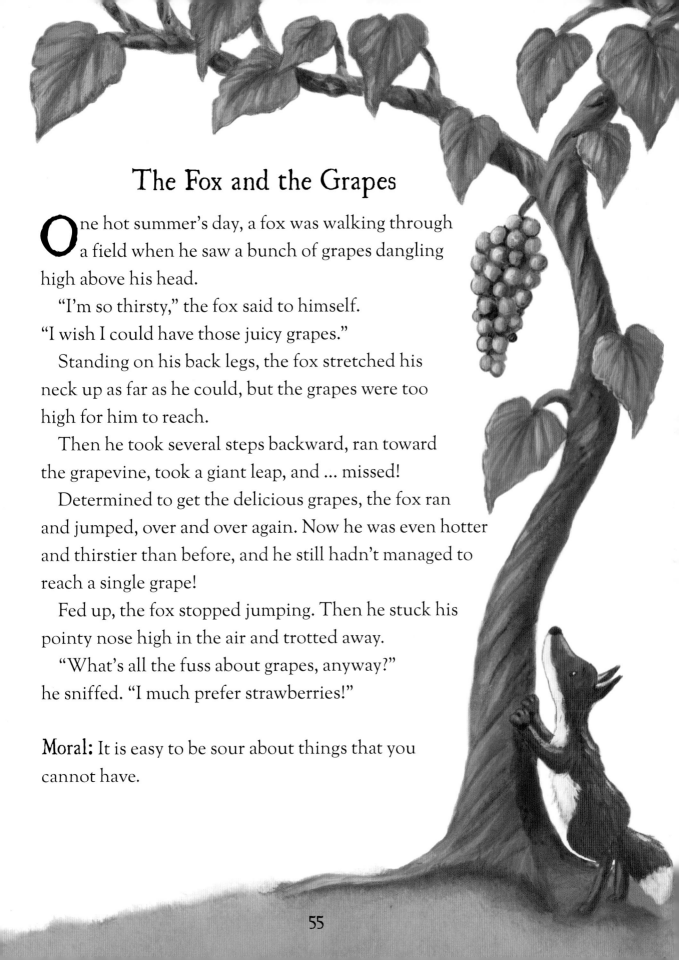

The Fox and the Grapes

One hot summer's day, a fox was walking through a field when he saw a bunch of grapes dangling high above his head.

"I'm so thirsty," the fox said to himself. "I wish I could have those juicy grapes."

Standing on his back legs, the fox stretched his neck up as far as he could, but the grapes were too high for him to reach.

Then he took several steps backward, ran toward the grapevine, took a giant leap, and ... missed!

Determined to get the delicious grapes, the fox ran and jumped, over and over again. Now he was even hotter and thirstier than before, and he still hadn't managed to reach a single grape!

Fed up, the fox stopped jumping. Then he stuck his pointy nose high in the air and trotted away.

"What's all the fuss about grapes, anyway?" he sniffed. "I much prefer strawberries!"

Moral: It is easy to be sour about things that you cannot have.

The Lion and the Mouse

Once upon a time, there was a huge lion who lived in a dark, rocky den in the middle of the jungle. When the lion wasn't out hunting, he loved to curl up in his den and sleep. In fact, as his friends knew, if he didn't get enough sleep, the lion became extremely grumpy.

One day, while the lion lay sleeping as usual,

Zzzzzzzzzzzzzzzzzzzzzzz!

a little mouse thought he'd take a shortcut straight through the lion's den. He lived with his family in a hollow at the bottom of a tall tree just on the other side of the lion's rocky home. He was on his way home for supper and didn't want to have to climb up and over the big boulders surrounding the den.

"What harm can it do?" he thought. "He's snoring so loudly, he'll never hear me."

As he hurried past the snoring beast, he accidentally ran over the lion's paw. With a mighty ROAR, the lion woke up and grabbed the little mouse in one quick motion.

"How dare you wake me up!" the lion roared angrily. "Don't you know who I am? I am King of the Beasts! No one disturbs my sleep. I will eat you for my supper." He opened his huge mouth wide.

Shaking with fear at the sight of all the lion's sharp, pointed teeth, the terrified little mouse begged the angry lion to let him go.

"Please, Your Majesty," he cried. "I didn't mean to wake you up. It was an accident. I was just trying to get home to my family. I'm too small to make a good meal for someone as mighty as you. Let me go, and I promise to help you one day."

The grumpy lion stared at the little mouse. Suddenly, he laughed loudly.

"YOU help ME?" he said scornfully, shaking his furry mane. "Ha! Ha! Ha! What a ridiculous idea! You're too small to help someone as big as me."

The little mouse trembled and closed his eyes as he waited for the terrible jaws to snap him up.

But to his surprise, the lion didn't eat him. Instead, he smiled and opened his paw.

"Go home, little mouse," said the lion. "You have made me laugh and put me in a good mood, so I will let you go. But hurry, before I change my mind."

The little mouse was very grateful. "Thank you, Your Majesty!" he squeaked. "I promise to be your friend forever, and I won't disturb you again."

As quickly as he could, the little mouse scurried home. What a story he would have to tell his children!

A few days later, the lion was out hunting in the jungle. As he crept stealthily through the lush undergrowth, he smelled something delicious. There, in a small clearing just ahead of him, stood a goat eating the juicy leaves and grass beneath a shady tree.

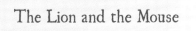

The lion circled the clearing, slowly crawling through the tall grass. He crouched low, ready to pounce on the unsuspecting goat ... when suddenly, a big net fell on him.

He was trapped in a hunter's snare!

The goat, bleating in terror, ran off into the jungle. The lion roared and tried to break free from the trap. But the more he struggled, the more he became tangled in the net. He was so angry—and a little bit scared, even though he would never admit that to anyone—that he let out the loudest of roars.

RROOAARR!

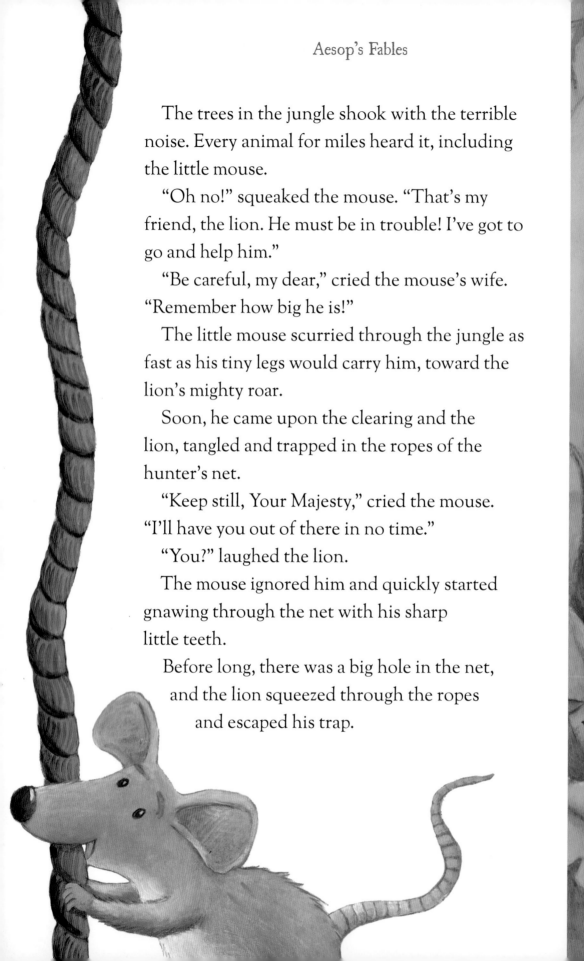

The trees in the jungle shook with the terrible noise. Every animal for miles heard it, including the little mouse.

"Oh no!" squeaked the mouse. "That's my friend, the lion. He must be in trouble! I've got to go and help him."

"Be careful, my dear," cried the mouse's wife. "Remember how big he is!"

The little mouse scurried through the jungle as fast as his tiny legs would carry him, toward the lion's mighty roar.

Soon, he came upon the clearing and the lion, tangled and trapped in the ropes of the hunter's net.

"Keep still, Your Majesty," cried the mouse. "I'll have you out of there in no time."

"You?" laughed the lion.

The mouse ignored him and quickly started gnawing through the net with his sharp little teeth.

Before long, there was a big hole in the net, and the lion squeezed through the ropes and escaped his trap.

The lion held out his giant paw toward the little mouse. "Thank you, my little friend," he said humbly, bowing his huge head. "I was wrong when I laughed at you and said that someone as small as you couldn't help me. You saved my life today, and I am truly grateful."

The little mouse smiled up at the lion. "You were kind enough to let me go before, and I promised I would be your friend forever," he squeaked. "It was my turn to help you."

Side by side, the big lion and little mouse walked back into the jungle. From that day on, the huge, mighty lion and the tiny, mighty mouse became the best of friends.

Moral: Little friends can prove to be great friends.

The Rat and the Elephant

One day, a small brown rat was traveling along the highway toward a big bustling town. The rat was in a bad mood because just that morning he had been caught stealing food from the café kitchen near his home, and the cook had chased him away. It wasn't the first time he'd been caught stealing food there. So, thinking that he might have better luck elsewhere, the rat packed up his things and set off down the highway to find a new place to live. He was very hungry and hoped that it wouldn't be long before he was enjoying a tasty meal.

He had been walking all morning and hadn't seen a single person on the road when suddenly, he spotted a huge crowd up ahead.

"What a nuisance!" scowled the rat. "That crowd is blocking my way. I'll have to push through, but it will slow me down." His stomach growled.

As he got closer to the crowd, he could hear music playing and people talking excitedly. He squeezed his way to the front, so that he could see what everyone was looking at. There was a royal procession passing by: At the front was the king riding on an elephant, and behind him were all his children and servants. Behind them, musicians were playing flutes and drums. The king's favorite pets were on the elephant's back with him: his dog, sitting up proudly in a golden basket, and his cat, lying on a crimson cushion.

The king and his children looked very fine, but it was the elephant that the crowd was staring at. It was a magnificent beast, tall and heavy, wearing a jeweled headdress, gold chains on its tusks, a garland of exotic flowers looped over its ears, and many gold bracelets around its huge feet.

"Look at the elephant!" exclaimed one man excitedly. "He's so tall."

"And so strong!" added a woman. "He could carry the royal palace itself on his back!"

"What a huge trunk!" called a little boy who was sitting on his father's shoulders.

The rat was not impressed. "I can't see what all the fuss is about. I'm just as great as that elephant," he said to himself.

The elephant lumbered on, uncoiling his long trunk and flapping his huge ears. The crowd clapped their hands.

"That elephant may be tall and strong," sneered the rat, "but I wouldn't want to carry a man on my back, even if he was a king. And why is an elephant's trunk so special? I have a neat pink nose that can sniff out food in even the deepest garbage can. That's much better than a trunk."

The elephant shook his head from side to side, and the chains on his tusks flashed in the sunlight.

"Ooooh!" roared the crowd. "Look at those amazing tusks!"

"Ha!" said the rat in disgust. "That elephant may have tusks, but can they cut a hole in a bag of grain or gnaw a tunnel through a wooden floor? I don't think so!"

"Daddy, Daddy!" cried the little boy again. "The elephant's skin is so wrinkly."

"What's good about wrinkles?" scoffed the rat. "I have silky brown fur all over, soft and warm and shiny. Thick, wrinkly skin? Yuck!"

No one in the crowd took any notice of the rat, of course, and that made him even angrier.

"What fools you are!" he squeaked at the crowd. "I'm just as good as that elephant in every way! He's slow and clumsy, and he's blocking the road. Why does he have the right to make me late for my dinner?"

He jumped up and down in anger.

The king's favorite pet cat happened to be looking into the crowd at that very moment and caught sight of the angry rat. She was feeling hungry and thought that the rat might make a tasty snack. So, quick as a flash, she jumped down from the elephant's back and raced across the highway and straight toward the distracted rat. At the last second, he noticed her swiping her paw toward him, and he ran far, far away from the town.

"I'm as great as an elephant, you know!" squeaked the rat as he ran. But the elephant feasted on a meal fit for a king that night, and the rat did not.

Moral: Thinking that you are important is not the same as being important.

The Crow and the Pitcher

One hot summer day, when there had been no rain for months and all the ponds and rivers had dried up, a thirsty crow was searching for a drink. At last, he spotted a pitcher of cool water in a garden and flew down to take a drink. But when he put his head into the neck of the pitcher, it was only half full, and the crow could not reach the water.

Now, the crow was a smart bird, so he came up with a plan—he would break the neck of the pitcher, then reach down to the water below.

Tap! Tap! Tap! The crow pecked the pitcher with his sharp beak again and again, but it was so hard and strong, he couldn't make even the tiniest crack.

The crow did not give up easily, so he thought of another plan. He would tip the pitcher over. The bird pushed and pushed as hard as he could, but the pitcher was very heavy, and it would not move at all.

The poor crow knew that if he did not get a drink soon, he would die of thirst. He had to find some way of getting to the water in the pitcher! As he looked around and wondered what to do, he saw some pebbles on the path, and he had an idea.

He picked up a pebble in his beak and dropped it into the pitcher. The water level rose a little. The bird got another pebble and dropped it in. The water rose a little more. The crow worked very hard, dropping more and more pebbles into the pitcher until the water was almost at the top.

At last, the bird was able to reach the water—and he drank and drank until he could drink no more. His clever idea had saved his life.

Moral: Little by little does the job.

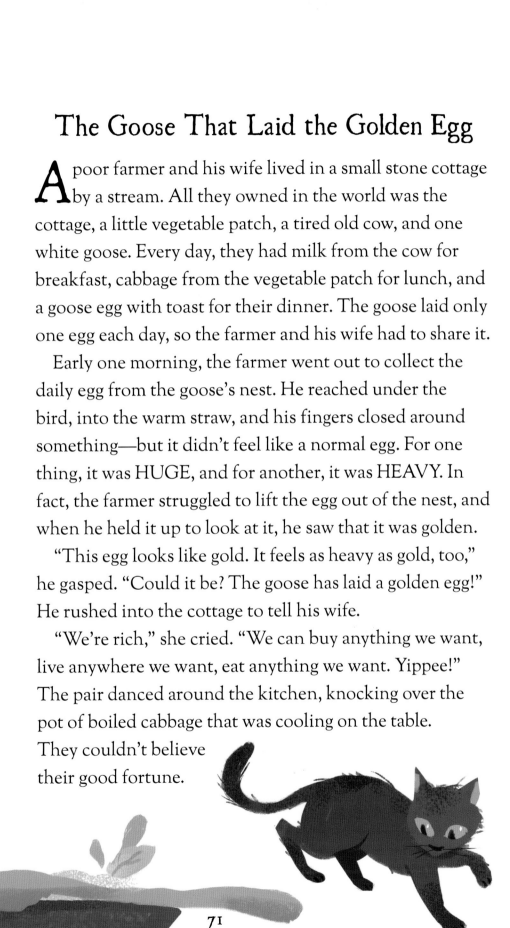

The Goose That Laid the Golden Egg

A poor farmer and his wife lived in a small stone cottage by a stream. All they owned in the world was the cottage, a little vegetable patch, a tired old cow, and one white goose. Every day, they had milk from the cow for breakfast, cabbage from the vegetable patch for lunch, and a goose egg with toast for their dinner. The goose laid only one egg each day, so the farmer and his wife had to share it.

Early one morning, the farmer went out to collect the daily egg from the goose's nest. He reached under the bird, into the warm straw, and his fingers closed around something—but it didn't feel like a normal egg. For one thing, it was HUGE, and for another, it was HEAVY. In fact, the farmer struggled to lift the egg out of the nest, and when he held it up to look at it, he saw that it was golden.

"This egg looks like gold. It feels as heavy as gold, too," he gasped. "Could it be? The goose has laid a golden egg!" He rushed into the cottage to tell his wife.

"We're rich," she cried. "We can buy anything we want, live anywhere we want, eat anything we want. Yippee!" The pair danced around the kitchen, knocking over the pot of boiled cabbage that was cooling on the table. They couldn't believe their good fortune.

Now, to have one golden egg is lucky, but that wasn't the end of the story. The goose laid another egg the following day, a third egg the day after, and on and on for weeks. The weeks turned into months, and still the goose kept laying those fabulous golden eggs.

The farmer and his wife lost no time in spending their newfound wealth. They bought a huge mansion to live in, they rode everywhere in a smart carriage pulled by six fine horses, and they didn't eat milk for breakfast, cabbage for lunch, and an egg with toast for dinner anymore. They ate only the finest foods prepared by a world-famous chef. They bought the goose a jeweled collar to wear and a red velvet cushion to sit on, which it liked a lot. It still laid only one egg a day, though.

Years passed, and the farmer and his wife got richer and richer. They had so much money that they didn't know what to spend it on. But that didn't stop them wanting even more.

One night, the farmer woke up suddenly and sat bolt upright in bed. He'd had a brilliant idea. It was such a good idea that he couldn't wait until morning to tell his wife. He woke her up.

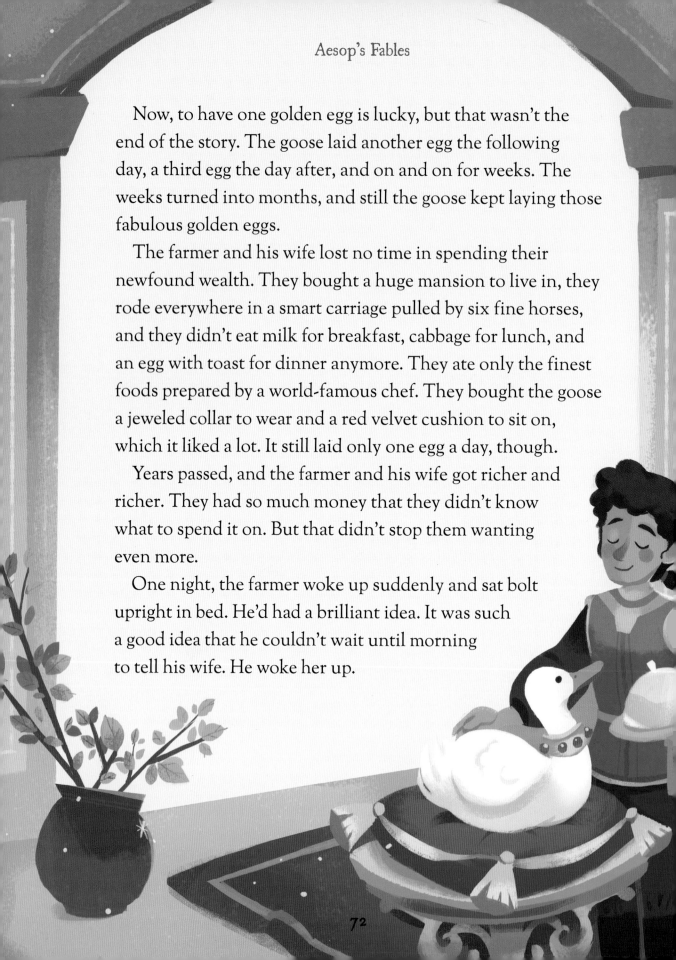

"I know how we can get even more gold," he told her gleefully. "Our goose lays only one egg a day, doesn't she? But she must have more golden eggs inside her, waiting to come out. If there are lots of eggs in there, and we could get them out together, think of all the money we would have!"

"I'm sure you're right, my love," replied his wife, giving him a big kiss on the cheek. "Let's get all those lovely eggs and spend all that lovely money as soon as we can!"

First thing the next morning, the farmer cut open the goose to find the golden eggs that he thought were inside her. But much to his disappointment, there were no more golden eggs in there. In fact, there were no more golden eggs at all, ever.

Without their golden eggs, the farmer and his wife began to run out of money. It costs a lot to live in a mansion with a carriage and a chef. It wasn't long before they had to sell the mansion and go to live in a stone cottage again. They had to sell the carriage, too, and send the chef away.

Soon, their lives were back to the way they had been before the goose started laying the golden eggs: They worked in the vegetable patch, milked the cow, ate cabbage and toast, with not even one egg to share between them.

In fact, their lives were worse than they were before, because the farmer and his wife couldn't forget how very SILLY they had been to be so greedy.

Moral: It is better to be happy with what you have than to be greedy for what you don't have.

The Fox and the Stork

Once upon a time, a fox decided to play a trick on his neighbor, the stork.

"Would you like to come and have supper with me?" he asked her one morning.

The stork was surprised by the invitation, because the fox had never been friendly to her before, but she happily accepted. He looked like a well-fed beast, and she was sure he would provide her with a good meal.

Every now and then, through the day, the stork caught the mouth-watering smell of the soup that the fox was preparing. By the time she arrived at his home, she was feeling very hungry—which was exactly what the fox wanted.

"Enjoy your meal," said the crafty fox, ladling the soup into a shallow bowl. Of course, the fox was able to lap his up easily, but the stork could only dip the tip of her bill into the soup. She wasn't able to drink a single drop!

"Mmm, that was delicious," said the fox when he had slurped up the soup. "I see you don't have much of an appetite, so I will have yours, too."

The poor stork went home feeling hungrier than ever and was determined to take her revenge on the sly fox for playing such a mean trick. So, the following week, she went to see him.

"Thank you for inviting me to supper last week," she said. "Now I would like to return the favor. Please come and dine with me this evening."

The fox was a little suspicious that the stork might want to get back at him, but he didn't see how she could possibly play a trick on him. After all, he was known for his cunning, and very few creatures had ever managed to outwit him.

All day long, the fox looked forward to his supper, and by the evening, he was very hungry. As he approached the stork's home, he caught the appetizing aroma of a fish stew and started to lick his lips.

But when the stork served the stew, it was in a tall pot with a very narrow neck. The stork could reach the food easily with her long bill, but the fox could only lick the rim of the pot and sniff the tempting smell. As much as he didn't want to, the fox had to admit he had been outsmarted—and he went home with an empty stomach.

Moral: Treat others as you would like to be treated.

78

Zeus and the Tortoise

The gods on Mount Olympus were famous for their fabulous parties. They would have a party whenever they had something to celebrate, and they celebrated a lot.

When the greatest god of all, Zeus, decided to get married, he wanted to have the very best party there had ever been.

He handed out invitations to all the creatures in the land, from the biggest horse to the smallest mouse. The animals were very excited. They had heard about the parties on Mount Olympus before. They all accepted.

"If it's anything like Zeus's parties in the past, the food will be delicious—and it never runs out," said a hairy dog.

"And there'll be dancing all day and all night," said an elegant flamingo.

"I love dancing!"

Everyone was excited about the party, except for Tortoise. Tortoise lived a quiet life. He liked to be at home, and he didn't go to many parties. So when all the other animals were discussing Zeus's invitation, he didn't join in. He just kept quiet.

The day of the party arrived, and the animals made their way to Zeus's palace. Through the golden gates and up the marble staircase they went to the front door, where Zeus welcomed them. Then they followed him through the door and into a vast dining room, where tables were laid with the finest foods that the animals had ever seen. There were grapes shining like jewels, melons the color of the sun, and towers of cakes in every flavor imaginable. Beyond the dining room was a ballroom, where an orchestra of harps and flutes were playing, and gods and goddesses were already dancing. Everything about the party was fabulous. The animals couldn't decide what to enjoy first!

Zeus was in a very good mood. All his animal friends were there, including the dog with his mouth full of cake, and the flamingo spinning on the dance floor with a handsome heron. Then Zeus frowned. Where was the tortoise? Zeus looked and looked, but Tortoise was nowhere to be found.

The day after the party, Zeus went to find Tortoise. Perhaps he had a good reason for not coming. Zeus found Tortoise at home, as always, sitting in the garden with his eyes closed and dozing in the sunshine.

"Why didn't you come to my party?" said the god. "Did you feel unwell?"

Tortoise opened his eyes.

"No, I am perfectly well, thank you, Zeus. I just didn't want to go."

Zeus's face turned red. "Everyone else was there aside from you," he said crossly.

"Yes, I know," said Tortoise. "But I don't like parties. I don't like music or dancing, and all that rich food would have given me a tummy ache. Besides, I like to be at home. I have everything I need here— in fact, I think that going out is a waste of time."

If Tortoise had apologized nicely, Zeus might have forgiven him. But he didn't. Zeus had worked hard to make the party special, and here was Tortoise telling him that it had all been a waste of time! Zeus was furious.

"You are very rude," said Zeus. "If that's how you feel, perhaps you would like to be at home all the time, forever!"

There was a flash of light, and a thunderbolt shot from Zeus's hand. It hit the tortoise—SMACK. Tortoise blinked in the bright light.

He felt strange, as if he had a heavy weight on his back.

"What have you done to me?" he gasped.

"You said that you wanted to stay at home," laughed Zeus, "so now you have your house on your back. You will carry it with you wherever you go."

Sure enough, the tortoise now had a hard, heavy shell on his back. It was so heavy that he could only move very slowly. He tried to look behind him and found that he could hardly move his head at all.

After Zeus left, the sun disappeared, and it started to rain. "I must go indoors," thought Tortoise miserably, "or I'll get wet." Then he realized that escaping from the rain was easy. All he had to do was tuck his head and his legs inside his shell.

"How lucky I am," laughed Tortoise. "I always said that I wanted to be at home all the time, and now I am! I'm dry and safe and just where I want to be."

Moral: There is no place like home.

The Wolf and the Crane

Once upon a time, a greedy wolf was gobbling up an enormous meal when he got a bone caught in his throat. The wolf tried coughing ... then he tried swallowing ... then he tried drinking, but the bone would not move up or down. It was really stuck, and he couldn't eat a thing. As the days passed, the wolf got thinner and thinner.

One morning, the wolf noticed a crane flying overhead, and he had an idea.

"You have such a wonderful long bill," he said to her, when she had landed. "You could do me a great service and save my life. I have a bone caught in my throat, so I cannot eat, and I am starving. With your long beak, you could reach down into my throat and pull the bone out for me."

The crane felt very nervous about putting her head into a hungry wolf's mouth. After all, he could be planning to eat her.

"I'd like to help," the crane replied, "but I'm afraid that you might bite my head off."

"Why would I do that?" the wolf replied innocently. "In fact, I'd be so grateful to you that I would give you a reward."

The crane was tempted by the thought of a reward, so she agreed to do as the wolf asked.

The wolf opened his mouth, and the crane reached down into his throat with her long bill. She was relieved to find that the wolf was telling the truth and that he really did have a bone stuck there. So she grabbed it with her beak and pulled it out.

As soon as the crane had pulled out the bone, the wolf turned around and began to walk away.

"Just a minute! What about my reward?" called the crane.

"I've given you your reward already," the wolf replied. "I let you take your head out of my mouth without biting it off, even though I am starving. You should be very grateful for that!"

Moral: Sometimes being helpful is its own reward.

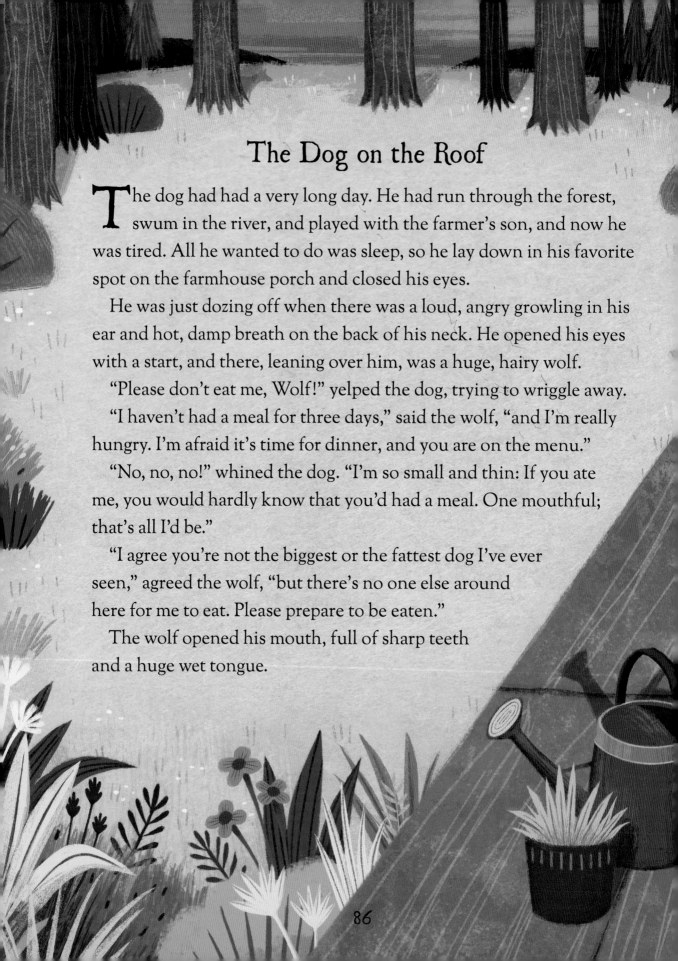

The Dog on the Roof

The dog had had a very long day. He had run through the forest, swum in the river, and played with the farmer's son, and now he was tired. All he wanted to do was sleep, so he lay down in his favorite spot on the farmhouse porch and closed his eyes.

He was just dozing off when there was a loud, angry growling in his ear and hot, damp breath on the back of his neck. He opened his eyes with a start, and there, leaning over him, was a huge, hairy wolf.

"Please don't eat me, Wolf!" yelped the dog, trying to wriggle away.

"I haven't had a meal for three days," said the wolf, "and I'm really hungry. I'm afraid it's time for dinner, and you are on the menu."

"No, no, no!" whined the dog. "I'm so small and thin: If you ate me, you would hardly know that you'd had a meal. One mouthful; that's all I'd be."

"I agree you're not the biggest or the fattest dog I've ever seen," agreed the wolf, "but there's no one else around here for me to eat. Please prepare to be eaten."

The wolf opened his mouth, full of sharp teeth and a huge wet tongue.

"Stop!" shrieked the dog. "What I meant to say was, don't eat me now. My owner is having a wedding feast on Saturday, and he will give me all the leftover food. This time next week, I will be so fat, my tummy will be tight as a drum and my legs as thick as tree trunks. If you come back then, I will be a proper meal for such a fine animal as yourself."

"Hmmm!" said the wolf thoughtfully. "That does sound tempting. All right, I will let you go now, but you must eat as much as you can at the feast and then be here waiting for me on this porch when I come back."

"It's a deal," said the dog.

A week is a long time for a hungry wolf, but at last the day arrived when he would have his meal of fattened-up dog. He ran through the farmyard and up to the farmhouse porch, but the dog was nowhere to be seen. The wolf was wild with hunger by this time, so he was in no mood for playing hide-and-seek with the dog.

"Where are you, Dog?" he growled. "You and I had an agreement: I would let you go, you would fatten yourself up at the feast, and then I would come back here and eat you. I've done my part, now you must do yours."

There was a long, loud yawn. The dog, who was asleep high up on the roof of the farmhouse, rolled over and scratched his tummy lazily. It was a big, round tummy now, very full of food.

"Oh, hello, Wolf," the dog said sleepily. "I won't come down right now, if you don't mind. I'm still so full from the feast that I just don't think I can move."

"B-b-but what about our agreement?" stuttered the wolf. "You said I could eat you, but I can't get to you up there on the roof."

The dog looked down at the wolf and smiled.

"Do you really think I'm going to come down there and let you eat me?" he replied. "You should have eaten me while I was thin, instead of waiting for me to get fatter."

The wolf was furious, but there was nothing he could do. He couldn't climb up to the roof to eat the dog, and the dog would not come down to him. He had no choice but to go home, his tummy rumbling all the way.

Moral: Learn from your experience.
It will help you in the future.

The Dog on the Roof

The Rooster and the Fox

There once was a wise old rooster who lived on a farm with his ten plump hens. Every day, as the sun rose, the rooster flew up to sit on a branch in a tall tree beside the farmyard gate. Sitting up there, he could see the whole farm and the countryside around it. This was very useful, because if any danger was nearby, he would see it. Once he had checked that the coast was clear, the rooster would take a deep breath, puff out his chest, and give an almighty COCK-A-DOODLE-DOO. This woke the hens and let them know that it was safe for them to come out into the yard. They had nothing to fear.

One morning, a fox was trotting past the farm, when he saw the rooster high up in the tree. The fox was hungry, and the rooster was plump and well fed—just the sort of tasty meal the fox was looking for. If he could lure the rooster to fly down from the tree, thought the fox, he could eat him for breakfast. And once he had gone, there would be no one to protect the hens, so the fox could eat them up, too. With this in mind, the fox trotted up to the farmyard gate. He knew he would have to be clever to trick the rooster, but he had a plan.

"Good morning," he said politely, looking up at the rooster. "Have you heard the good news?"

The rooster looked down at the fox. He knew that the fox was cunning, so he guessed that this was some kind of trick.

"No," he said cautiously. "What good news are you talking about?"

The fox smiled knowingly. "The king has announced that all the animals and birds in the land must be friends," said the fox. "It's forbidden for them to eat each other. Isn't that wonderful? Come down out of your tree, and I'll tell you more about it."

The rooster tipped his head to one side.

"Is that so?" he said. "I'm very pleased to hear it. So if I came down out of this tree and spoke to you, you wouldn't jump on me and eat me up?"

"Oh no," said the fox sweetly. "That would be completely against the law. Please come down so that we can be friends."

The rooster sat on his branch and looked out over the countryside. Then he blinked and blinked again, as if he had seen something very interesting in the far distance.

"What are you looking at?" said the fox, who was feeling hungrier every minute.

"I can see a pack of dogs running through the forest," said the rooster. "They're running very fast, and they seem to be coming this way."

"Goodness, how time flies!" said the fox nervously. "I've just remembered that I'm late for an appointment. Please excuse me, Rooster, I have to go at once."

"Oh, please don't go," said the rooster. "I'm coming down right now. I want you to tell me all about the wonderful announcement. The dogs will be here soon, too, and we can all discuss it together, now that there's nothing for you to fear."

"Oh, no," said the fox, now shaking with fear. "I really must go. Those dogs don't know about the announcement yet, so I'm afraid they will eat me." With that, the fox ran off and disappeared across the fields on the other side of the farm.

The rooster watched him go from his seat in the tall tree. Then he puffed out his chest and gave the most almighty COCK-A-DOODLE-DOO! It was safe once again for the hens to come out into the yard.

Moral: Do not believe everything you are told.

The Donkey and the Pet Dog

A long time ago, a man lived in a small cottage with his pet dog. He kept a donkey in a stable at the end of his yard, to help him work the land and carry heavy loads. The donkey had to work very hard, but he always had a warm bed to sleep in at night and plenty of oats and hay to eat.

The donkey couldn't help but notice that the dog didn't have to do any work. The dog played all day and his master was always stroking him and giving him treats to eat. The donkey was very jealous of the dog's lazy and luxurious life.

One day, the donkey decided he'd had enough.

"It's not fair!" he shouted. "I work hard every day, while that dog gets all the attention for doing nothing!"

He galloped into the cottage. Kicking up his hooves and braying loudly, he tried to jump onto the man's lap as he had seen the dog do. But of course, he was too big. He broke the chair and all the dishes on the table. The man was so angry that he chased the donkey out of his home.

"Don't ever show yourself here again!" cried the man.

The poor donkey hung his head in shame.

98

"Oh, if only I'd been satisfied with what I already had," he sighed unhappily, as he trotted away. "I'll have to find a new home now."

Moral: Do not try to be someone you are not.

The Cat and the Hens

Tabby the Cat was a large, fluffy, orange-and-white farm cat. When he wasn't sleeping in the soft hay in the barn, he spent his time catching mice for supper. Tabby had a good and easy life, but every day was exactly the same. Tabby was bored of chasing mice. He was bored of having mice for breakfast, lunch, and dinner.

"Oh, I wish I could eat something else for a change," Tabby whined to his friend Wily Fox.

"Why don't you try bird?" said Wily.

"Oh, I would like to," sighed Tabby, "but I can't catch one! They always manage to fly away."

Tabby didn't tell Wily Fox that the real reason he couldn't catch a bird was that he was rather lazy and that it was too much effort to run and jump around.

"What about slugs and snails?" suggested Wily.

"Ugh!" cried Tabby. "Too squishy and crunchy at the same time!"

"Well," sighed Wily reluctantly, "I suppose you could try hen." Hen was his favorite dish, and he wasn't sure if he wanted to share the farmer's plump, juicy hens with anyone else, not even a friend. "Just make sure you only take what you need, and leave plenty for me." With a flick of his splendid red tail, Wily Fox slunk away to make his own dinner plans.

Tabby set off for the chicken coop right away. "If Fox can catch hens, then surely I can, too," he said to himself. "I'm just as clever as he is!"

He crept silently through the bushes until he came to a tall fence that surrounded the chicken coops. Inside, he could see lots of plump, juicy hens pecking seeds on the ground. He raised his head and sniffed ... delicious!

But how was he going to get inside? The fence was too high for him to jump over, and the little gate was locked.

As Tabby crouched in the bushes pondering the problem of how to catch a hen, the farmer and his son walked by and unlocked the gate.

"Can you collect the eggs from the coops in the corner?" called the farmer to his son, quickly closing the gate behind him again. "I'm just going to check on Mildred and Henrietta. They haven't been laying eggs this last week, and I'm a little bit worried about them. I might have to call out the vet to have a look at them."

When he heard this information, Tabby grinned to himself. He knew how he could get inside the chicken coop. He had the perfect plan!

Crawling away quietly, Tabby went back to the farmyard. The kitchen window in the farmhouse was open, so he slipped inside and crept into the hallway. The farmer and his family kept their coats and hats there on a stand. Tabby grabbed the smallest jacket he could find and one of the farmer's old flat caps and ran back to the barn. He lay down in the hay, dreaming of a delicious chicken supper, while he waited for dusk to fall.

At dusk, as the animals on the farm settled down for the night, Tabby slipped on the jacket and pulled the cap low over his face. Standing on his back legs, he casually strolled over to the gate of the chicken coop.

"Knock, knock!" cried Tabby.

"Who's there?" clucked a little white hen.

"It's just me, the vet," replied Tabby. "The farmer asked me to check Mildred and Henrietta."

The little hen moved closer to the gate. "Oh yes, they haven't been well," she clucked sympathetically. "Come in." And she reached up to unlock the gate.

"Stop!" cried a big red-and-black hen. "Something's not quite right."

The Cat and the Hens

103

Several hens had gathered by the fence to see what was going on.

"Look!" said the big red-and-black hen. "The vet has whiskers and a twitching orange-and-white striped tail!"

"And sharp teeth and claws!" squawked another hen.

"You're not the vet!" clucked the hens loudly. "We've seen you creeping around the farm before. You're a cat!"

"And cats eat creatures like us!" cried the little white hen.

"Oh, don't be silly," purred Tabby softly. "I only eat mice, and I've come to make Mildred and Henrietta feel better."

"Well, that's very kind of you, sir," replied the clever red-and-black hen. "But I think they will feel much better if we don't let you in. So please just go away and leave us alone. You're not welcome here."

"That's no way to treat your visitors!" muttered Tabby, but he knew he had been outsmarted by the clever hens. Throwing off his disguise, he ran away back to the barn, twitching his orange-and-white tail.

"I guess it will be mouse again for supper, after all," he sighed loudly.

Moral: Uninvited visitors are often most welcome when they are gone.

The Eagle, the Jackdaw, and the Shepherd

Jackdaw loved shiny objects. His nest was littered with bottle caps, coins, pieces of glass, and gleaming pebbles. He was very proud of his collection, and every day, he liked to add something new to it.

Just that morning, Jackdaw had found a beautiful, sparkling ring. As he settled back in his nest to admire his latest treasure, he saw a huge eagle soaring high above his treetop home. Jackdaw carefully placed the ring on the straw in his nest and turned to watch the eagle swooping and gliding on the warm breeze.

"That is some bird!" Jackdaw cawed in admiration. "What magnificent wings! Oh, how I wish I could be as powerful as him."

As he watched, the eagle suddenly dived downward toward a meadow full of sheep. The eagle swept past the shepherd and grabbed a lamb in his strong talons. The shepherd ran toward them, shouting and waving his stick, but it was no use. The eagle gripped the lamb firmly by its soft, woolly coat, and off he flew, up, up, and away, higher and higher, until he disappeared over a stand of trees in the next valley.

Jackdaw gazed into the distance, dreaming of soaring and swooping like the mighty eagle.

"Dream on! You'll never be like the eagle," said a mocking voice, breaking into Jackdaw's daydream.

Jackdaw turned to see Magpie sitting on the edge of his nest.

"I'm just as fine a bird as him," said Jackdaw angrily.

"What? You think you could swoop down with those small raggedy wings and grab a lamb with your little stubby claws?" laughed Magpie.

"Of course, I could!" boasted Jackdaw. "I could even snatch a large ram if I wanted to!"

"Go ahead, then!" mocked Magpie. "I bet you that sparkly ring that you can't."

Jackdaw puffed out his feathers. How dare Magpie tell him he wasn't as good as the eagle!

"Fine," he cawed. "If I lose, you get my ring, but if I catch the ram, you have to bring me something glittery and shiny."

Magpie grinned. "It's a deal."

Jackdaw flapped his wings and flew down to the meadow. He could hear Magpie laughing high up in the tree.

"I'll show him!" he muttered to himself.

Spying a large ram on the hillside, he launched himself through the air and dived down onto the ram's huge back. Jackdaw grabbed at the ram's wiry wool with his claws.

"Here I go!" he cried, rising into the air. But all that was hanging from his claws was a tiny bit of wool.

The ram kept on grazing happily. He hadn't even noticed Jackdaw. Jackdaw dropped the wool and plunged back down onto the ram's back. This time, he grabbed the wool harder and pulled with all his strength. But nothing happened.

Jackdaw could not budge the ram. He tugged and tugged at the wiry wool. He flapped his wings up and down and up and down, but still he could not lift the ram at all.

Up in the treetop, Magpie laughed and laughed.

The more he laughed, the angrier Jackdaw became. Flapping his wings furiously and cawing loudly, Jackdaw tugged and jumped up and down, getting his claws more and more tangled in the ram's thick fleece, until finally, he couldn't move at all.

Meanwhile, hearing all the noise and commotion that Jackdaw was making, the shepherd wandered over to the ram.

"Silly old bird!" laughed the shepherd. "What are you trying to do?"

Jackdaw stopped struggling. He knew there was no point now.

The shepherd gently grabbed Jackdaw around his belly and untangled his claws. Then he clipped his wings and put him in a sack.

"I can't have you fooling around with my flock," he said. "I'll take you home. You'll make a great pet for my children."

Poor Jackdaw! As the shepherd carried him home, he could hear Magpie cackling in the distance. And to add to his embarrassment, he'd lost the bet, and now Magpie would take all his precious treasures from his nest.

When the shepherd got home, he put Jackdaw on the table and called to his children.

"Look what I have brought you," he said.

"What kind of bird is it, father?" cried the children.

"Well," chuckled the shepherd, "I call it a jackdaw, but he seems to think he is a mighty eagle!"

Jackdaw hung his head in shame. He had learned his lesson: Being stubborn and too proud had cost him his freedom.

Moral: Do not try to act more important than you are.

The Fox and the Goat

One hot day, a thirsty fox was searching for something to drink. At last, he found a well in a farmyard. He stuck his nose over the edge, but the water was too far down. Very carefully, he balanced on the side, trying to reach the cool, clear water. But though his nose was so close that he could smell it, he still couldn't quite reach the water.

The fox made one last try, stretching out his tongue with all his might. SPLASH! He toppled right in.

The sides of the well were so slippery that when the fox tried to climb out, he just kept sliding back down. He was stuck!

After a while, a goat came by looking for a drink. He was surprised to see the fox in the water.

"What on earth are you doing down there?" he asked.

"Just cooling down," replied the fox. "The water in this well is the best for miles around. Why don't you jump in and try it?"

The goat was very hot and thirsty, and the water did look very refreshing, so he jumped in to join the fox.

"You're right!" said the goat, taking a long drink and relaxing in the water. "It's lovely and cool down here."

Soon, the goat decided that it was time to go on his way.

"How do we get out?" he asked.

"That is a little problem," the fox admitted. "But I've got an idea. If you stick your legs out, you can wedge yourself in the well. Then I can climb on your back and jump out."

"That's all very well, but what about me?" the goat bleated.

"Once I've climbed out, I can help you get out," the fox explained.

So the goat wedged himself against the walls of the well, and the fox clambered onto his back and leaped out.

"Thank you," laughed the fox, as he turned to leave.

"Hold on! What about me? How am I going to get out?" cried the goat.

"You should have thought about that before you jumped in," replied the sly fox, and off he ran.

Moral: Always look before you leap.

The Frogs Who Wanted a King

It was another noisy day at the pond. The morning air was filled with the sound of angry croaking, and the clear blue water was rough with ripples and waves. The frogs were quarreling again.

All over the pond, they were pushing and shoving, puffing up their chests, and shouting at the tops of their voices. They were arguing about everything: who could sit on which lily pad, who had the most warts, and, most of all, who could croak the loudest. The noise was deafening.

One old green frog, who was trying to get some sleep under a rock, covered his ears, but he could still hear everything. Exasperated, he took a deep breath and shouted "BE QUIET!" in a voice so loud that all the other frogs stopped croaking at once in surprise.

"Listen, everyone," said the old frog. "We must stop all this arguing. It's horrible to listen to, and it never ends. There must be another way to settle our quarrels."

There was silence on the pond.

"I have an idea," he said. "What if we ask Zeus to choose a king for us? That king could solve all our arguments."

The other frogs thought this was a great plan and croaked in agreement.

"I'm going to see Zeus right away," said the old frog. "Who's coming with me?"

The great god Zeus lived high up on Mount Olympus, in a palace in the clouds. When the frogs arrived, he was sitting on his cloudy throne, eating grapes from a huge golden bowl.

"Your majesty," said the old frog politely. "We frogs cannot live in peace together, and we need someone to lead us. Please, can you find us a king?"

"Hmm," said Zeus, looking down at the frog. "What kind of king are you looking for?"

"Someone who is a good listener," called out a bold young frog.

"And someone we can look up to," added another.

Zeus chuckled. "These frogs have no idea what it's like to have a king. Let's see if they like the one I choose for them," he thought.

"Go back to your lake," he told them, "and I will send you a king."

The frogs hopped home to their pond and waited. Suddenly, there was a flash of light and a gust of wind, and a large wooden log landed in the water with a splash.

At first, the frogs were frightened, but when the water was calm again, they were excited. They had a king!

"Amazing!" they croaked. "Look how strong he is and how quietly he listens."

One by one, the frogs approached the log and politely asked for help to solve their disagreement. The log, of course, said nothing. It wasn't long before the frogs gave up and started sitting on their "king" instead, as if he was just an ordinary log.

The frogs visited Zeus again.

The Frogs Who Wanted a King

117

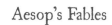

"Your majesty," began the old frog politely. "Thank you for the king you sent us, but unfortunately, he wasn't what we wanted. Please, can you send us a different one, who answers when we speak to him and doesn't just sit around all day?"

Zeus smiled to himself, but he agreed to send them another king.

The frogs went back to their lake, and this time Zeus sent a large brown eel in a flash of light. As first, the frogs were delighted. The eel was friendly and talkative, not silent at all like the log. He seemed to be the perfect king. But after a while, they realized that he was actually too friendly. Once he started giving his advice, it was impossible to keep him from talking!

The frogs went back to Zeus a third time. The god was resting and was very irritated to see them again.

"Let me guess ... you want a different king?" he asked crossly. "Go back to your pond at once, and I will send you another one. But this will be your last."

The frogs went home and waited for their new king. They were excited: What would he be like? Strong and friendly but not too talkative, they hoped, and someone they could look up to.

They didn't have to wait very long. With a blinding flash of light and an icy gust of wind, a large gray heron appeared. All the frogs were terrified because they knew that herons ate frogs. The heron's beady eyes glinted, his sharp beak snapped, he swooped low over the water, and the frogs ran for their lives. They hid in the mud, under the rocks, and anywhere else they could find, and they never showed their faces on the surface of the pond again. From then on, they tried very hard to solve their disagreements themselves!

Moral: Be careful what you wish for.

The Hare Who Had Many Friends

Once upon a time, a young brown hare lived in the fields beside an old farm. She lived a very good life: She had lots of fresh green grass to eat, lots of sunshine to warm her fur, and lots of good friends.

"My friends are so important to me," the hare thought every day. "They would always be there to help me if I needed them. I am very lucky."

One spring day, the hare was out in the fields, nibbling the fresh green grass, when she heard a most unpleasant sound in the distance. It was the sound of hunting dogs, barking excitedly as they ran through the countryside.

"Oh, no," thought the hare. "They'll surely catch me. I must get away as fast as I can."

Far off in the distance, the dogs yapped with glee. They were definitely coming closer.

"What shall I do?" gasped the hare, trying to think how she could escape. Then she had an idea. "I'll ask my friends for help. If I can go over the hill behind the farm and across the stream, I know I'll be safe, and I'm sure that one of my friends will be able to carry me there."

So the hare dashed to the farmyard, where she knew that her friend the horse would be. He was just the kind of friend that you could rely on when there's trouble.

"Horse, please, can you save me?" panted the hare. "The hunting dogs are coming, and I need to get away. If you will carry me over the hill and across the river, I will be safe."

The horse was one of the hare's best friends, but when he heard her request for help, he shook his head.

"I can't help you today, Hare. I'm taking the farmer's wife to town, so I'm really very busy. I'm sure the bull will help you if you ask him."

The hare didn't have time to be upset, so off she ran to find her friend the bull. Luckily, he was nearby, beside the farmyard gate.

"Bull, my dear friend, please, can you save me? There are hunting dogs running this way, and I must escape from them. Will you carry me over the hill and across the river to safety?"

The bull was a very good friend of the hare, but when he heard her request for help, he frowned.

"I can't, I'm afraid. The farmer is taking me to the country show today, where I will certainly win a prize. I'm really very busy. Why don't you ask the goat? I'm sure he will help you."

The hare was surprised that the bull couldn't help her, but luckily, she had other friends to ask. So off she ran to look for the goat.

She didn't have far to go to find him, which was just as well, because she could hear the barking of the dogs getting closer. He was in the meadow beside the farmhouse, quietly chewing a thistle.

"Goat, please, can you help me?" panted the hare. "The hunting dogs are after me, so will you carry me over the hill and across the river to safety?"

The goat was old, and he rarely went out, and he certainly NEVER ran anywhere. So, he sadly shook his head.

"I can't, Hare, but ask the ram. He's big and strong—I'm sure he'll help you."

The hare could hear the dogs clearly now, only two fields away. Shaking with terror, she darted back past the farmhouse and across the yard, to find the ram, drinking from the water trough.

"Ram, you must help me!" gasped the poor hare, and she explained about the hunting dogs and how all her other friends were too busy to help her.

"I would if I could," said the ram, "but I'm having my fleece trimmed so ..."

The hare didn't wait to hear the rest. She had one more friend, the calf, so she raced to the barn to find him.

"Calf!" she sobbed. "I have asked all my other friends, and none of them will help. You're my last hope!"

"Oh, Hare, if none of the others will help you, I'm afraid I really can't. I'm much too young, you see."

By now, the hunting dogs were bounding up the lane toward the farm, yelping at the tops of their voices. There was no time to lose.

"All I can do is run for my life," said the hare to herself, so off she raced, over the hill and across the river, and found a place to hide until the dogs gave up the chase. She was safe at last, and she never saw her so-called friends ever again.

Moral: A friend who does not help when you are in trouble is not a true friend at all.

The Wolf in Sheep's Clothing

Once upon a time there was a big, bad wolf. He lived in a cave at the foot of a steep, rocky mountain. A shallow, slow-flowing brook ran past Mr. Wolf's cave, and on the other side of it was a green, green meadow. The meadow belonged to a farmer, and this was where the farmer grazed his flock of sheep.

Now, as you know, a wolf's favorite dish is sheep. And to have so many sheep so near was fantastic for Mr. Wolf. Well, it would have been, except that Mr. Wolf could never catch a single sheep because the farmer or his son was always guarding the flock.

Poor Mr. Wolf! The smell of sheep wafted through the air into his cave day and night. He dreamed of delicious sheep suppers and feasting on the flock.

Every day, Mr. Wolf tried to come up with a cunning plan for how he could get past the farmer and his son and catch even just one of the large, juicy sheep. But every day, his wily ways failed.

One day, feeling particularly fed up and very hungry, Mr. Wolf prowled up and down his side of the brook, watching the sheep grazing happily in the meadow on the other side. As he came to a bend in the brook, where the water was very shallow and a tangle of thornbushes hid him from view of the meadow, something woolly caught his eye.

"I wonder what that is?" he said to himself. The woolly object smelled rather bad, but he tugged at it until it came loose from the bushes. It was a large sheepskin! The farmer must have discarded it, and it had washed down the stream and gotten caught in the bushes.

Mr. Wolf grinned to himself. He had a brilliant idea!

"I will disguise myself as a sheep in this old skin," he cackled, "and then I can sneak into the meadow. The farmer will never even know that I am there."

Mr. Wolf dragged the smelly sheepskin back to his cave and waited for dusk to fall. When the light started to fade, and Mr. Wolf could just make out the shapes of the sheep in the meadow opposite and hear their soft bleating, he pulled the sheepskin over his own furry coat and crept out of his cave.

"At last," he sighed, padding along the bank of the brook, "a yummy sheep supper for me tonight!"

When he came to the thornbushes, where the water in the brook was just a tiny trickle, Mr. Wolf crossed the stony riverbed. Silently, he sneaked into the meadow and slyly slipped in among the flock.

The sheep didn't seem to notice the newcomer, even though he was larger than they were. They continued to graze happily on the lush green grass as the sun set.

Mr. Wolf couldn't believe his luck! He was almost dizzy with the delicious smell of sheep, and he had to stop himself growling for joy in anticipation of the wonderful feast he was going to have that evening.

As he walked among the sheep, pretending to nibble on the grass, Mr. Wolf glanced around him. He couldn't see the farmer, but he could hear him pacing up and down along the edge of the flock, muttering something to himself. Mr. Wolf wanted to make sure the farmer was as far away as possible before he made his move.

"I must be patient," Mr. Wolf thought. "The wait will be worth it."

Then he spotted a large sheep grazing slightly apart from the rest of the flock, by a stand of trees on the edge of the meadow.

"That one will do nicely," he whispered hungrily, and slowly started to move toward it.

Unbeknown to Mr. Wolf, the farmer always counted his sheep first thing in the morning and last thing at night, to make sure he hadn't lost any during the day.

"... twenty-eight, twenty-nine, thirty, thirty-one ..." counted the farmer.

The farmer was a few steps away from Mr. Wolf. Mr. Wolf held his breath and kept still, waiting for the farmer to move past. Once he had moved safely down the line of sheep, then Mr. Wolf would pounce!

But suddenly the farmer stopped.

"Thirty-one?" he said. "I have only thirty sheep!"

And quick as a flash, spotting the extra-large sheep, he hooked it with his shepherd's crook and dragged it toward him.

"You're not one of my sheep!" shouted the farmer. "I'll have you for my supper!"

Mr. Wolf, realizing that his plan had failed and that he could not fool the farmer, twisted and tugged and wriggled free of the sheepskin caught in the farmer's crook, and he ran as fast as his legs could go, back across the brook.

"No sheep supper for me again," he growled sadly when he reached his cave. "Or ever!"

Moral: Things are not always what they seem.

The Fox's Tail

One day, a fox was out walking when he heard a loud snap and felt a sudden pain in his tail. The poor fox had been caught in a hunter's trap. He looked behind him and saw that his tail was completely stuck. No matter how much he struggled, he just couldn't free it.

"Help!" he shouted. "Ouch!" he cried. "Owwww!" he howled. But no one came to help him.

At last, the fox pulled and pulled with all his strength and managed to break free, but when he looked back, he saw that his tail had been left behind in the jaws of the trap.

"What will all the other foxes think when they see me?" thought the fox. "They'll all laugh at me. I don't even look like a fox without my tail. It's so embarrassing!"

For days, the fox hid away in his den and only came out at night when no one could see him. Then he came up with an idea. He called a meeting of all the foxes in the area.

The foxes gathered in a clearing. Sure enough, as soon as they saw the fox without his tail, they started to laugh.

"I've called you together to tell you about my wonderful discovery," the fox announced, struggling to be heard above their laughter. "Over the years, I've felt that my tail was nothing but a nuisance. It was always getting muddy, and when it rained, it got all wet and took ages to dry. It slowed me down when I was hunting, and I never knew what to do with it when I was lying down. So I decided it was time to get rid of it, and I can't tell you how much easier it is to move around without all that extra weight dragging along behind me. I cut my tail off, and I recommend that you all follow my example and do the same."

One of the older foxes stood up. "If I had lost my tail like you, I might have agreed with what you are saying," he said. "But until such a thing happens, I will be very happy to keep my tail, and I am sure everyone else here feels the same."

The other foxes all stood up and proudly waved their tails in the air as they walked away.

Moral: Be wary of suspicious advice.

The Peacock and the Crane

Every day, Peacock liked to parade up and down the riverbank near his home, so that he could show off his splendid shimmering tail feathers to anyone that happened to be passing by.

And every day, Peacock admired his reflection in the river.

"Look at me!" he would cry. "I'm so handsome, no other creature can compare to me!"

One fine morning, when Peacock took his usual majestic stroll along the riverbank, a crane, who was catching fish in the shallow waters at the edge of the river, stopped to watch him. The sunlight glinted off the dazzling blues and greens and yellows of Peacock's long tail feathers, which swept the ground behind Peacock as he proudly strutted past.

Crane stared in wonder at the beautiful sight. Her own feathers were dull and plain.

"Oh, wouldn't it be lovely to have such splendid and colorful feathers!" she sighed wistfully.

Peacock turned to admire his reflection in the river and saw Crane staring at him.

Looking down his beak, he said scornfully, "Yes, I'm not surprised you are admiring me. If I had such dreary feathers as yours, I wouldn't be happy either!"

Poor Crane didn't know what to say. She bowed her long neck down to the water to hide her shame.

"And as for your lanky body and funny, long neck and skinny, knobbly knees, well …" crowed Peacock nastily. He fanned out his glimmering tail feathers around him. "I'd be embarrassed!"

Crane looked up at the intricate patterns of Peacock's feathers. It was like hundreds of sparkling rainbow-colored eyes were looking back at her, staring at her own plain, ugly feathers.

"You'll never be as beautiful as me," said Peacock, and with a haughty swish of his gorgeous tail, he continued his stroll.

"It's true," thought Crane sadly to herself. "Look at everyone admiring Peacock. No one looks at me like that."

Flapping her long, strong wings, Crane rose into the air and flew off to perch in a nearby tree. Deep in her heart, she knew she shouldn't feel envious. After all, Peacock was rude and mean, and not many of the other animals really liked him. Yet, she couldn't help looking at him.

All that day, and for several days afterward, Crane watched Peacock as he moved around. She was careful to stay out of his way, but she couldn't help overhearing his boastful comments or notice the rude way in which he treated everyone.

"You could use my feathers to make a gorgeous gown fit for a queen!" Peacock said to a flock of sparrows one day.

"If you want to brighten up your dull black feathers, you could decorate them with some of my old ones!" Peacock said to a crow another time.

As she watched, Crane noticed that at the end of each day, as the sun dipped behind the horizon, Peacock made his way to the same tree. There, with a big show of flapping his wings and an awkward jump, he flew clumsily up to a low branch to roost for the night.

Crane was curious, so one evening, she decided to visit Peacock in his tree.

"Every night, you roost on a low branch in this tree," she said. "Why don't you fly up higher? You'd be much safer, especially since the fox has been prowling around here the last few days."

With a haughty turn of his head, Peacock replied, "I can't fly any higher. My splendid tail is too long and heavy."

Crane was surprised. "Oh dear," she replied. "What a shame. You mean to say that you've never soared through the sky on a beautiful sunny day? It is such a wonderful feeling!"

"No. Why would I want to?" snapped Peacock.

"And you've never flown through a velvet night with the light of the moon and the stars shining down on you?" continued Crane. "It's amazing!"

"No!" shouted Peacock. "Why would I waste time doing that? If I want to see something amazing, I only have to look at my own beautiful feathers or gaze at my glorious reflection!"

Suddenly, Crane smiled to herself. She couldn't believe how vain and arrogant Peacock was. All week, she had been worrying about her own dull feathers and comparing herself to Peacock, but now she realized that she didn't need to.

"Dear Peacock, it is true that you have beautiful feathers," she said, "and that my black-and-white feathers are plain. But at least I can use my dull feathers to fly with and soar through the sky!"

"How dare you speak to me like that!" cried Peacock. "You are just jealous of me."

Crane spread her broad wings and flapped them gently. "I certainly don't envy you anymore," she said. "I can soar freely, while you are forever stuck on the ground!"

With that, Crane flew up into the night sky and away under the splendid, silvery light of the moon.

Moral: Appearances can be deceiving.

The Tortoise and the Eagle

There was once a tortoise who was very unhappy with his life. He hated crawling around on the ground all the time and was very jealous of the birds who could soar high into the sky. He was sure that if he could just get up into the air, he would be able to fly as well as they could.

One day, the tortoise was sitting on a rock by the seashore, when an eagle flew down and landed nearby.

"Will you teach me how to fly?" the tortoise asked the eagle.

"Don't be so silly," said the eagle. "How could you fly? You don't have any wings."

"I'm sure I could fly, if I could just get off the ground," the tortoise insisted. "You are a big, strong bird. You could carry me into the sky, and once I'm up there, you could tell me what to do and let me go. Then I could fly away."

"Listen," the eagle explained, "I have been flying around in the sky for many years, and the only creatures I have ever seen up there all have one thing in common: They have wings!"

But the tortoise wouldn't give up. "I will give you all the treasures in the ocean if you will teach me to fly," he promised the eagle.

Finally, the eagle got tired of listening to the tortoise begging and pleading.

"All right," he agreed. "I will take you up into the sky, and when we get there, I will let you go, and you can try to fly."

The tortoise was delighted that he would be leaving the ground at last. The eagle carried him all the way over the ocean. They were so high that the tortoise could almost touch the clouds.

"Are you ready?" the eagle said. "Stretch out your legs and flap them."

"Yes, yes, let me go," the tortoise cried impatiently.

So the eagle let go of the tortoise, who stretched out his legs and flapped them furiously, as he had been told.

Can you guess what happened next? The tortoise dropped like a stone and fell ... down, down, down to the ground below, where he was happy to stay forevermore.

Moral: Demanding your way does not mean that it will work out.

The Cat and the Mice

Mungo, Martha, and Morty lived in a little mouse hole behind the baseboard in a bakery. Their cozy home was always warm, and the wonderful smell of freshly baked bread wafted through the air. The three little mice were never hungry. They feasted day and night on an endless supply of delicious bread and pastry crumbs, which fell to the shop floor while the baker worked.

Mungo was the oldest and wisest of the three mice. He had lived in the bakery for many years and had seen several bakers come and go. He had also known times when food was scarce.

Martha and Morty, on the other hand, had only recently moved in. They were young and didn't know much about the big, wide world outside of the mouse hole. Life was easy and fun, and food was always plentiful.

Every evening, after the baker closed the shop, the three mice would scurry out of their safe mouse hole and gather up all the crumbs. Then they would fill their pantry with the tasty morsels.

Sometimes, if the baker was in a hurry to get home, he forgot to close the pantry door properly. As soon as the baker climbed the stairs at the back of the bakery to his apartment above, Mungo, with Martha and Morty following close behind, would sneak through the crack and into the pantry, where the shelves were filled with cakes and buns and pastry swirls, and loaves of bread in all shapes and sizes. There, the three little mice would eat and eat the sweet and savory treats, until their tummies were ready to burst.

One morning, after the mice had particularly indulged themselves, the baker noticed that food had disappeared from his pantry. He followed a trail of crumbs and saw that they led to a tiny hole in the baseboard.

"Oh no!" he cried. "Mice! I'll have to get myself a cat."

The very next day, he bought himself a large grayish-brown tomcat.

"Good Puss," said the baker that evening, as he prepared to leave the shop. "You make sure those pesky mice don't steal my bread."

Puss purred happily. Mice were his favorite snack, and he was looking forward to catching his supper. Padding stealthily across the floor on his velvet paws, Puss stationed himself near the mouse hole and sat down to wait.

Inside the mouse hole, the three mice were planning their usual evening excursion.

"Martha and Morty," squeaked Mungo, "you check behind the counter, and I'll go and see if the pantry is open."

Giggling and pushing each other playfully, the two young mice popped their heads out of the hole and sniffed the air.

"Mmm," sighed Martha. "I can smell doughnuts tonight."

"Yummy!" squeaked Morty. "My favorite. Perhaps the baker dropped some behind that furry thing on the floor."

"Furry thing?" Mungo grabbed Morty's tail firmly. "Stop!" he hissed quietly.

"But I love doughnuts," whined Morty, trying to inch forward. "Why can't I go?"

"Cat alert!" whispered Mungo. "Look, over there!"

Morty and Martha had never seen a real cat before.

"I'm hungry!" whined Martha. "We can just sneak past him, can't we?"

"No!" said Mungo firmly. "Cats are dangerous creatures, and they like eating mice for their supper."

The two young mice looked at Mungo in horror. "What are we going to do now?"

"We'll have to wait until he falls asleep," replied Mungo.

But Puss had no intention of falling asleep. He'd seen the flurry of activity by the mouse hole and realized that the mice were not going to risk coming out of their home while they could see him waiting to pounce.

"I'll have to come up with a cunning plan," Puss thought to himself.

As he glanced around the shop, Puss noticed some sacks of flour on a shelf. The sacks were the same color as his fur.

Puss grinned a wicked grin. "Purr-fect!" he purred. "I'll climb up on that shelf and pretend to be a sack of flour. The mice will think I've gone and come out of their mouse hole. Then ... POUNCE! I get to have my supper!"

Puss made a lot of noise, as if he were leaving the room. Then he quietly jumped up onto the shelf, lay down, and pretended to be a sack of flour.

Back at the mouse hole, Morty peered out and looked around.

"The cat's gone!" he whispered.

"Are you sure?" asked Mungo. "They don't usually give up that easily."

"Doughnuts, here we come!" cried Martha, and she darted across the floor to the counter.

"Martha, get back here at once!" shouted Mungo. He had seen something gray and furry lying on the shelf, and he was sure it had just twitched.

"What's wrong?" said Martha, scurrying back to the hole as fast as her little legs would carry her.

"There!" said Mungo, pointing to the shelf.

"Oh, don't be silly," laughed Morty. "It's just a sack of flour!"

"Sacks of flour don't twitch," replied Mungo. "It's a trick. I'll show you."

Mungo popped his head out of the hole and shouted, "You can lie there as long as you like, Mr. Cat, pretending to be a sack. But I can see your tail moving. I know your tricks, and we are not coming out."

Puss knew the game was up. The mice would never come out while he was in the room.

"All right," he grumbled. "You caught me. I'm going." And with another swish of his tail, he jumped off the shelf and sauntered up the stairs at the back of the bakery.

"But, Mungo ... how did you know?" asked Morty.

"I've witnessed the tricks of many cats in my time," replied Mungo. "And one of the most important things I've learned is that you can NEVER, EVER trust a cat."

Moral: Do not be fooled by someone who has proven to be dangerous.

The Lion and the Fox

Lion was not happy. He stared at his reflection in the sparkling water of the watering hole. His fur was dusty and dull, his once splendid mane was matted and limp, his sharp teeth were worn down, and his claws were cracked and stained. He felt tired. The bones in his body ached, and he had no energy. And to top it all off, he was hungry!

"Grrrrr!" he growled unhappily. "I'm getting old and useless. How am I going to catch my dinner? I'm exhausted all the time and too slow to hunt."

As Lion lay by the watering hole feeling sorry for himself, he noticed three birds drinking from the water nearby. Normally, most animals kept their distance when they saw Lion. But the little birds didn't seem to be afraid of him.

Lion chuckled to himself. He had a great idea.

"Those birds obviously think I'm harmless because I look so old and feeble," he muttered. "Well, we'll see! If I can't hunt for my dinner, I can get it to come to me!"

Lion slowly ambled over to his den. With a loud and sorrowful groan, he lay down.

"Oh, poor old me!" he cried. "I feel terribly sick. I'm so weak, I can hardly move!"

The little birds drinking at the watering hole turned when they heard Lion's sickly moans. Bravely, they flew over to his den.

"Oh, your Majesty," they chirped. "Whatever is wrong? You don't look very well."

"No, I'm very sick," sighed Lion dramatically. "I haven't felt like eating for days, and I can barely drag my tired old body down to the watering hole for a drink."

"You poor thing," chirped one of the birds. "Come to think of it, you do look rather pale."

"Yes," groaned Lion. "If only I could have some company, I'm sure I'd soon start to feel better. Perhaps you could tell the other animals that I'm ill and that I'd love to have some visitors."

The little birds felt very sorry for Lion.

"I'll go and tell the other animals right away," said one of the birds, and off she flew. The second little bird followed her.

The third little bird said, "Let me check your temperature." And she hopped onto Lion's nose.

With a quick move of his paw, Lion grabbed the unsuspecting bird, and shoved her into a sack that he kept in his den.

"Yum, you will be tasty but not very filling," said Lion, as he tied the sack closed. "I'll need to catch something else."

Lying back down at the entrance to his den, Lion let out another shrill groan.

"The pain! The misery!" he cried. "I'm sick and all alone!"

"What's the matter?" asked a small deer from a safe distance. She had been grazing nearby when she heard all the groaning.

"I'm very unwell," lied Lion. "I feel so weak."

"Yes, you do look terrible," replied the deer. "Let me check your temperature." And she walked right up to Lion.

With a quick move of his paw, Lion grabbed the startled deer and shoved her into the sack with the bird.

"You will certainly make a delicious snack," growled the lion. "But I think I will still need something else to fill me up." He closed the sack and lay down once again.

By this time, the news that Lion was unwell had spread.

"I heard that you were sick," said a monkey, leaping down from the tree where he had been eating a banana. "Here, have these bananas, they will make you feel better."

"That's very kind of you," groaned Lion. "Would you be so kind as to put them in that sack for me, since I can't get up?"

"Of course," said Monkey, reaching into the den for the sack.

With a quick move of his paw, Lion grabbed the kind monkey and shoved him in the sack, too.

"You will make a superb supper," laughed Lion. "And I can have the bananas for dessert!"

Throughout the rest of the day, Lion pretended to be sick. One by one, the animals came to visit him. And one by one, he shoved them in his sack.

At last, as the sun was dipping behind the horizon, a clever fox sauntered over to Lion's den.

"Oh, Fox, thank goodness you are here!" whispered Lion. "My throat is so sore. I think there is something caught in it. Could you have a look?"

Fox looked at Lion and then looked at all the paw prints outside Lion's den. All of them were leading into the den, but there were none coming out again.

Inside the den, Fox could see an enormous sack that seemed to be wriggling.

"I'll take a look at your throat," said Fox, "but you need to close your eyes and keep very still."

Lion grinned to himself and opened his jaws, ready to snap up Fox.

As soon as Lion's eyes were closed, Fox crept quietly into the cave and opened the sack.

"You can open your eyes now, I'm all done. Everything looks fine!" Fox cried.

Lion opened his eyes just in time to see Fox and all the animals running away from the den, as fast as their legs would carry them.

Lion let out a loud, angry roar. "No, come back! You're my dinner!"

When the animals were far away from Lion's den, Fox turned to them.

"You're safe now. But don't fall for Lion's tricks. Next time, you'll end up as his dinner!"

Moral: If you are wise, you will watch out for signs of danger.

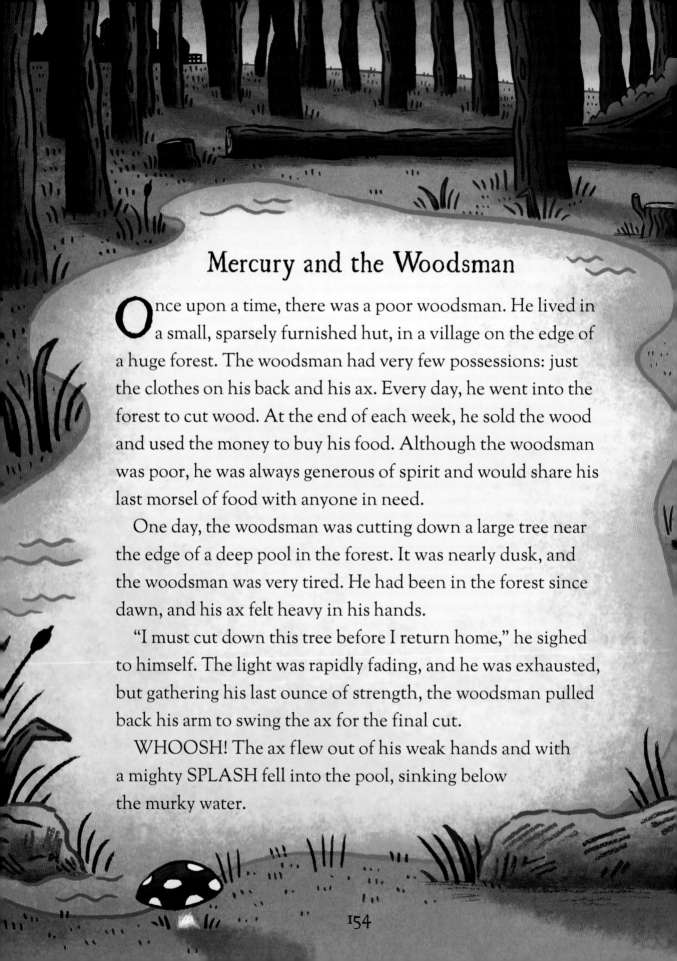

Mercury and the Woodsman

Once upon a time, there was a poor woodsman. He lived in a small, sparsely furnished hut, in a village on the edge of a huge forest. The woodsman had very few possessions: just the clothes on his back and his ax. Every day, he went into the forest to cut wood. At the end of each week, he sold the wood and used the money to buy his food. Although the woodsman was poor, he was always generous of spirit and would share his last morsel of food with anyone in need.

One day, the woodsman was cutting down a large tree near the edge of a deep pool in the forest. It was nearly dusk, and the woodsman was very tired. He had been in the forest since dawn, and his ax felt heavy in his hands.

"I must cut down this tree before I return home," he sighed to himself. The light was rapidly fading, and he was exhausted, but gathering his last ounce of strength, the woodsman pulled back his arm to swing the ax for the final cut.

WHOOSH! The ax flew out of his weak hands and with a mighty SPLASH fell into the pool, sinking below the murky water.

"Oh no!" cried the woodsman in despair. "What am I going to do?"
He didn't own another ax, and he couldn't afford a new one.
"How am I going to make a living now?" Weeping, the poor,
tired woodsman sank to the ground.

Suddenly, there was a flash of light in the gathering gloom of the forest, and the god Mercury appeared before the distraught woodsman.

"Sir, why are you crying?" asked Mercury, kindly.

The woodsman wiped his eyes and stared at Mercury. He had never seen a god before and wasn't sure how to address such a presence.

"I- I- I dropped my ax in that pool," he stammered. "It was all I had."

"Don't worry," replied Mercury, and with an agile leap, the god dived into the deep pool.

The woodsman stared in wonder as Mercury rose to the surface of the water, holding a shining gold ax above his head.

"Is this your ax?" Mercury asked the woodsman.

"No," answered the honest woodsman.

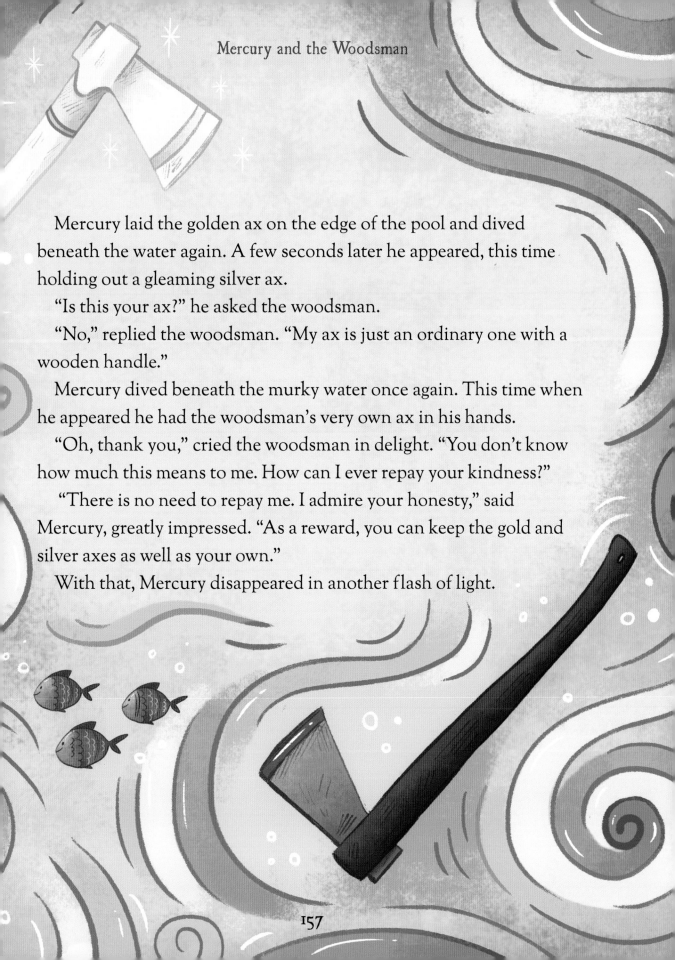

Mercury laid the golden ax on the edge of the pool and dived beneath the water again. A few seconds later he appeared, this time holding out a gleaming silver ax.

"Is this your ax?" he asked the woodsman.

"No," replied the woodsman. "My ax is just an ordinary one with a wooden handle."

Mercury dived beneath the murky water once again. This time when he appeared he had the woodsman's very own ax in his hands.

"Oh, thank you," cried the woodsman in delight. "You don't know how much this means to me. How can I ever repay your kindness?"

"There is no need to repay me. I admire your honesty," said Mercury, greatly impressed. "As a reward, you can keep the gold and silver axes as well as your own."

With that, Mercury disappeared in another flash of light.

The happy woodsman gathered up the axes and returned home. He would be able to sell the gold and silver axes for lots of gold coins, and he would never have to worry about replacing his own ax, or worry about money for food again.

Soon, the story of the woodsman's good fortune spread through his village.

"If poor Thomas can be so lucky," several of the other woodmen said, "then we should seek the same good fortune!"

So, over the coming days, the other woodmen traveled into different parts of the forest. Hiding their own axes under bushes or in the branches of tall trees, they pretended they had lost them and called on Mercury to help them.

"Kind Mercury!" wailed one woodsman. "Please help me find my precious ax."

"Oh, most gracious of gods," wept another. "My family will starve if I don't find my ax."

And of course, Mercury, who always responded to a cry for help, appeared to the woodmen. And every time, he showed each woodsman a glittering gold ax and asked him if it was his ax. All the woodmen replied that it was the very ax that they had lost.

But Mercury didn't give any of them a golden ax. Instead, he scolded them for their greed and dishonesty, and he sent them back home without anything. When they returned the next day to look for their own plain wooden-handled axes, they were nowhere to be found! Only the honest woodsman still had his own plain ax, and so much more.

Moral: Honesty is the best policy.

The Mouse and the Weasel

One day, a hungry mouse came across a basket of corn in a barn. There was a lid on the basket and a brick on top to keep out mice and rats, but the little mouse was starving. He was determined to get to the corn.

The mouse ran around and around and up and down the basket, until he found a narrow space between the strips of wood. Normally, the mouse would never have been able to squeeze through such a tiny hole, but he was so thin by now that he just managed to wriggle his way into the basket.

The mouse was so hungry that he ate, and ate, and ate. And then he ate some more. At last, he felt satisfied and burrowed his way back through the corn, until he found the space in the basket again.

But the hole suddenly looked very, very small—and the mouse was feeling very, very fat! In fact, his stomach was three times as big as it had been when he had squeezed his way in.

The mouse pushed his head through the hole and wriggled. It was no use. He couldn't get through. So he tried to pull his head back in again, only to find that he was completely stuck. He couldn't move backward or forward.

Just then, a weasel passed by. He saw the mouse's head sticking out of the basket and guessed what had happened.

"I know what you've been doing," laughed Weasel. "You've been stuffing yourself with food, and now you are stuck. It's your own fault. I don't have any sympathy for you, I'm afraid! You will just have to wait there without eating until you are thin enough to get out again."

And that's exactly what the greedy little mouse had to do.

Moral: Greed often leads to misfortune.

The Eagle, the Cat,
and the Wild Pig

On the edge of the forest, there was a large old oak tree. At the top of the tree lived an eagle and her three chicks. The eagle loved living in her bright, sunny nest, and the chicks loved it there, too.

At the bottom of the tree lived a mother pig and her six striped piglets. The mother pig loved living in her cool, dark den among the tree roots, and the piglets loved it there, too.

These two neighboring families lived happily in the oak tree. The eagle's chicks squawked and flapped their wings in the branches at the top, and the piglets squealed and chased each other around the roots at the bottom, while their parents watched them lovingly.

Then, one day, a cat moved into a hollow in the middle of the tree. She lived alone, with no kittens of her own, and she didn't like it when the chicks and the piglets disturbed her peace and quiet. It wasn't long before she decided that her neighbors had to move out.

First, she climbed up the tree to speak to the eagle.

"Aren't you afraid to have that mother pig living below you?" she said, her eyes wide with fear. "This morning, I saw her digging around the roots. I think she's trying to dig up the tree, and when it falls, what will happen to you and your chicks?"

"That is terrible!" said the eagle nervously. "Perhaps we should speak to the mother pig and try to make her change her mind?"

"You are braver than me," said the cat, shaking her head. "She has such sharp tusks that I would be afraid of getting too near. No, all we can do is stay in our homes, you in your nest and me in my hollow. If we stay still, let's hope the tree won't fall down."

The eagle thought this was a good idea, so she and her chicks climbed into the nest, and they sat there together, as still as statues.

Next, the cat climbed down to the bottom of the tree to speak to the mother pig.

"Aren't you afraid to have that eagle living above you?" said the cat, the fur standing up on her neck. "This morning, I heard her say that the next time she sees you go out into the forest, she will swoop down and gobble up all your piglets."

"That is awful!" said the mother pig anxiously. "Maybe if we talk to her together, we can make her change her mind?"

"You are braver than me," said the cat. "Her beak is as sharp as a knife: She could eat us on the spot! No, all we can do is stay in our homes. If she doesn't see us, perhaps she will forget about eating us."

The mother pig thought this was a good idea, so she rounded up her piglets right away. Then they all squeezed into their den and stayed there, not making a sound.

The cat was very pleased with herself. Her plan was working perfectly. All she had to do now was wait.

The Eagle, the Cat, and the Wild Pig

The eagle was so terrified that the tree was going to fall down, that she didn't move a muscle for two whole days and nights. Neither did the chicks. They were hungry and thirsty, but they couldn't go out. It was too dangerous.

The mother pig was so frightened that the eagle was going to eat her piglets, that she didn't go out for two whole days and nights. Neither did the piglets. They were hungry and miserable, but they couldn't leave. It was too dangerous.

By the end of the second night, the eagle could bear it no longer.

"We've loved living here," she sighed, "but we can't live in fear anymore. While it's still dark, and the mother pig can't see us, we must go and find a new home."

So quickly, quietly, the eagle and her chicks left their nest at the top of the tree and flew off deep into the forest.

Down at the bottom of the tree, the mother pig had also had enough.

"We've loved living here," she sighed, "but we can't stay any longer. While it's still dark, and the eagle won't see us, we must go and find a new home."

So secretly, silently, the mother pig and her piglets left their den and ran off in the other direction.

The cat, who was watching from her hollow, smiled to herself.

"Success!" she thought. "I have the tree all to myself. Those silly animals never knew that they'd been tricked!"

Then the silence and the darkness closed in around the cat, and she suddenly felt lonely.

"What am I going to do now?" she wondered.

Moral: Sometimes you should be careful what you wish for.

The Lion and the Statue

Once upon a time, there was a young man named Omar, who lived with his grandfather in a small house in the forest. Beyond the dense trees, there was a vast grassy plain. Each day, Omar would go into the forest to hunt for food. There were plenty of nuts and berries and rabbits and small deer, so he and his grandfather never went hungry.

Omar had heard about the huge, fierce lions that prowled the plains outside the forest. He loved listening to his grandfather's stories about the hunters from the local towns and villages, who boasted of their prize lion catches and how the other townsfolk honored them for their courage and strength.

"Oh, grandfather, I wish I were as brave as those hunters," sighed Omar one day, "but I'm terrified of lions!"

"Ah, Omar, don't you worry," said Grandfather. "We all have different skills, and you are a fine young man just the way you are."

"But to be stronger than a mighty lion!" said Omar. "That's truly amazing."

"Well, only if you want to catch a lion," chuckled Grandfather. "And remember, sometimes people exaggerate their bravery, so don't always believe what you hear. These hunters aren't all like Hercules."

"Who's Hercules?" asked Omar.

"He was an ancient Greek hero, the son of the god Zeus," explained Grandfather. "He had extraordinary strength and courage. The story goes that Hercules managed to stop the monstrous Nemean lion, who terrorized the people of Nemea. Many warriors had tried before him, but their mortal weapons could not pierce the lion's golden fur, and their armor couldn't protect them from its claws, which were sharper than swords."

"That lion sounds terrifying!" shuddered Omar. He had never seen a real lion up close, but he knew they had huge claws and scary sharp teeth. "I wouldn't like to bump into it on a dark night!"

Grandfather laughed. "Well, you can see his statue instead, if you like. Perfectly safe!"

"What do you mean?" asked Omar.

"The hunters have put up a statue of Hercules fighting the Nemean lion, in a clearing just outside the village on the other side of the forest," replied Grandfather.

"What's it for?" asked Omar.

"To remind them of their strength, courage, and skills in catching lions," explained Grandfather. "They hold a festival there once a year."

That night, Omar dreamed he was in ancient Greece, fighting the huge Nemean lion alongside Hercules. He was a brave warrior, and the people thought he was a hero! When he woke the next morning, Omar packed some bread and cheese in a cloth.

"Grandfather, I can't stop thinking about the story of Hercules and the lion," he said. "I must go see the statue today."

"Just make sure you are back before dark," said Grandfather, and he waved to Omar as he set off on his adventure.

Omar went into the forest. After several hours of walking, he felt tired, so he decided to sit down for a rest. He found a shady spot under a big baobab tree and was just about to take a bite of his bread, when he heard a terrible noise, like someone was in a lot of pain.

"Oh no!" Omar thought. "What is that?" Quivering a little, he turned toward the noise.

"I must be brave like Hercules," he muttered to himself.

As he peered around a tree, to his surprise and horror, he saw a huge lion. He was about to turn and run, when he realized that the lion was caught in a trap.

The lion is trapped, reasoned Omar, so he can't get me. Cautiously, he walked over.

"Please help me!" roared the lion. "I promise I won't hurt you if you set me free."

Remembering the story of Hercules, Omar said, "Of course. I'm not afraid of you, because as you know, man is stronger and mightier than a lion."

Although he was in pain, the lion scoffed. "That's ridiculous! How can you be stronger than me?"

"I can prove it," replied Omar, freeing the lion from the trap. "I'm on my way now to see a special statue. Come with me, and you'll see what I mean."

The lion was grateful to be free from the trap, so he decided not to eat Omar for supper and followed him into the undergrowth.

After a while, Omar and the lion came to a clearing. There in the middle, as his grandfather had described, was the statue.

"See!" said Omar triumphantly, pointing at the statue. The sight of Hercules defeating the lion made him feel unusually brave. "The King of the Beasts doesn't stand a chance!"

"Ha, ha, ha!" laughed the lion. Omar looked confused.

"A man made that statue," chuckled the lion. "If lions could make statues, it would have been quite a different scene. Hercules would have been squashed under a huge paw!"

And with a mighty roar, the lion ran off into the trees. Omar turned to look at the statue once more, thinking about the lion's words, before he, too, started his journey back home.

Moral: The version of a story depends on the point of view of the teller.

The Dog, the Rooster, and the Fox

Dog and Rooster lived on a farm. They were best friends. They both worked hard—Dog rounding up the sheep and keeping the farmer company, and Rooster waking up everyone in the morning and looking after the hens.

One day, after the pair had done their usual jobs, Dog padded over to the chicken coop and called out to her friend.

"Rooster," called Dog. "Would you like to go on an adventure?"

"What do you mean?" crowed Rooster.

"We both work so hard, I think we deserve a little holiday," replied Dog. "There's so much to see beyond the farmyard gates. Let's go and explore!"

Rooster was a rather cautious fellow. "Do you think that is a good idea? Will we be safe?" he worried. "I've heard that there are foxes out there in the big, wide world, and that their favorite dish is hen and rooster pie."

"Don't worry, my friend, you'll be safe with me," said Dog. "I'm not afraid of a fox. And I certainly won't let one bake you in a pie!"

Rooster smiled at his friend. It would be nice to go outside the farm for a change.

"All right, let's go!" he cried. "Who's afraid of a fox? Not me!"

The two friends set off on their adventure.

After a while, they crossed a stream and came to a grassy meadow, full of flowers, at the edge of a wood.

"There's so much space out here!" cried Dog.

"And look at all these beautiful flowers!" sighed Rooster.

"Let's play for a while," said Dog, and she ran off through the grass, jumping and barking for joy.

"I think I'll rest here," called out Rooster. "Be sure to bark loudly if you see a fox!"

"Don't worry!" shouted Dog. "I won't let any fox make you into a pie!"

Rooster sighed. Perhaps Dog was right. He should stop worrying and enjoy the adventure.

"Wait for me!" he called, and he flapped after Dog to play in the meadow.

Rooster and Dog were having so much fun that they didn't realize how much of the day had gone by, and soon, it was dusk.

"All that playing has made me hungry," said Dog.

"Me, too," replied Rooster. "It'll be dark soon. Let's get something to eat quickly and then find somewhere safe to sleep for the night."

"We can get some nuts and berries in the woods and then find a tree to sleep in," said Dog happily.

The two friends entered the woods. It was dark, and there were lots of strange creaking noises. Rooster felt a little afraid, but he didn't want to look like a coward in front of his friend, so he followed Dog along the shady path.

After a while, they came to a huge tree that had a hole hollowed out of it at the bottom.

"This is perfect," said Dog. "You can roost on that branch up there, and I can curl up in this hollow and keep guard."

Rooster was just settling down to sleep on his branch when something flitted past his head.

"Hey! Cock-a-doodle-doo! What was that?" he crowed.

From her cozy hollow below, Dog smiled. "It was only a bat, you silly thing! Good night."

"Oh, I thought it was a fox coming to make me into a pie!" said Rooster.

"I told you I won't let any fox make you into a pie," said Dog. "Go to sleep. I'll protect you. The fox won't even know you are up there, unless you keep making that noise!"

"Thank you, my friend," said Rooster. "Good night." Soon, he was fast asleep.

The next morning, as the sun came up, Rooster stirred on his branch.

"COCK-A-DOODLE-DOO!" he crowed loudly, forgetting that he wasn't home on the farm.

Suddenly, he heard a low growl nearby.

"Good morning, up there!" said sly Fox.

Rooster looked down.

"Oh, what have I done?" he thought to himself. "I've made too much noise, and now the fox is going to make me into a pie!"

"Aren't you going to invite me up?" grinned Fox.

"I wasn't expecting any visitors," crowed Rooster nervously. "You'll have to come back later when I've straightened up a little."

"Oh, I don't mind a little mess," said Fox. "I'd really just like to visit with you and meet my new neighbor."

Rooster thought for a moment, and then, remembering the words of his friend, he sighed loudly.

"Oh, all right. Go around to the door at the bottom of the tree, and my porter will let you in," he said.

Fox couldn't believe his luck. Humming a happy tune about rooster pies, he strutted around to the hollow at the bottom of the tree ... and came face-to-face with Dog.

"You'll have to get past me!" growled Dog fiercely.

Fox was terrified of dogs, and quick as a flash, he ran away as fast as his legs would carry him, never to be seen again.

From the safety of his branch, Rooster called out, "You can't trick me, Fox!"

"Let's go home," said Dog, smiling at her friend.

"Thank you, dear Dog, for saving me," cried Rooster. "Yes, let's go. I've had enough adventures to last me a lifetime!"

Moral: Those that try to deceive should expect their comeuppance.

The Explorers and the Bear

Once upon a time, there were two merchants, Peter and Ivor, who lived in an old city that was nestled halfway up a steep mountain.

Peter and Ivor were best friends. They had met each other many years before in the city's bustling marketplace where they both worked, Peter as a cloth merchant and Ivor as a spice trader, and they had been firm friends ever since. The two men had had many adventures together over the years.

One day, Peter asked Ivor if he wanted to go on a journey with him. He needed to visit a port city by the sea, on the other side of the forest, to collect some fine silk cloths. The journey would take him several days, and he didn't want to travel alone.

"It would be good to have some company on my trip," Peter said to Ivor. "And I can't think of anyone that I'd rather travel with than you, my dearest friend."

"I'd be honored," said Ivor. "And perhaps I can pick up some spices while we are there."

The two merchants set off early the next morning. The day was cold, but Peter and Ivor hardly noticed the chill in the air, as they chatted away, telling stories and enjoying each other's company.

The road to the port city went through a dark forest at the bottom of the mountain.

It was getting late by the time the two men reached the edge of the forest.

"Perhaps we should find somewhere to rest for the night," said Ivor. "It'll soon be dark, and I know that there are bears in the forest."

Ivor was terrified of bears, and he especially didn't care to meet one in the dark!

Peter was also scared of bears, but he didn't want his friend to know.

"Oh, don't worry," he laughed loudly. "You don't need to be afraid. Many years ago, when I was traveling alone through some woods, I met a bear. I fought him, and he ran away!"

Ivor was impressed by his friend's story. "Wow! How brave of you," he cried.

Ivor didn't want Peter to think he was a coward, so he said, "In that case, let's keep going, as I'm in such fine company!"

Peter nodded nervously, and the two merchants entered the forest. The trees grew close together, forming a dark canopy, and it was very hard to see the road in the growing gloom.

"Tell me all about your battle with the bear," said Ivor, fighting down his fear, as their footsteps echoed loudly in the quiet of the night forest. A sliver of moonlight filtered through the thick trees, casting scary shadows around the men.

"It was a huge bear, at least three times bigger than me," exaggerated Peter. "But I calmly picked up a large stick, and I fought it off. I think it was actually scared of me ..."

Suddenly, there was a loud crash, and a huge bear came lumbering out of the trees, sniffing the air, with its sharp teeth glinting in the moonbeams.

Peter and Ivor froze where they stood, but the bear had seen them. It raised its giant body onto its back legs and slowly moved toward them.

"Argh!" screamed Peter. He ran to the nearest tree and scrambled up it as fast as he could.

Ivor was still frozen to the spot. "What are you doing?" he whispered. "Quick! Come down and fight it, or it will eat me. You fought off that other bear, so you can do it again!"

From the safety of the high branch, Peter looked down at his friend, silently trembling and shaking his head.

"Well, at least pull me up," cried Ivor. "There's room on that branch for both of us."

"No there isn't," whispered Peter, too scared to try. "You'll have to find somewhere else to hide."

Meanwhile, the hungry bear had moved closer to Ivor.

"What shall I do?" Ivor thought to himself. The bear was so close now, he could feel its hot, rancid breath on his face. Then he remembered hearing somewhere that bears don't eat something that is already dead, so he dropped quietly to the ground and lay as still as he could.

A moment later, Ivor felt the bear sniffing him. He could feel its fur touching his skin.

"It's going to get me," Ivor thought, as drops of the bear's saliva fell onto his neck. His heart pounded faster and faster.

Then, as suddenly as he had appeared, the bear moved away, lumbering back into the dark forest.

For a few moments, Ivor couldn't move. Then, shaking all over, he got up, feeling lucky to be alive. Peter jumped down from his hiding place in the tree.

"What did the bear say to you?" Peter asked.

"What do you mean?" replied Ivor. He could hardly look at Peter, he was so angry with him for leaving him to face the bear on his own.

"I saw him whispering in your ear," said Peter.

Ivor thought for a moment. Then he said, "He said that a man who leaves his friend to face danger on his own is not a real friend."

With that, he turned back the way they had come, leaving Peter to make the rest of the journey on his own.

Moral: Only a true friend will face danger with you.

The Wind and the Sun

One sunny but cold fall day, the Sun shone down on the earth below and sighed happily.

She could see people strolling down streets or working outside, children playing in parks, boats sailing on sparkling water, cows and sheep grazing in fields, and birds sitting in the trees, cheerily singing their merry songs.

"What a wonderful sight," said the Sun, as she shone brightly. "I will certainly enjoy my journey across the sky today."

As she gazed across the clear blue sky, a sudden burst of cold air blew across her face and sent clouds scurrying along her path.

"Out of my way!" growled the Wind, racing past the Sun. "No time to waste. I've got work to do!"

"What are you up to?" the Sun called out.

"See those trees down there? I'm going to blow all the leaves off!" roared the Wind.

He blew and blew and blew so hard that the branches of the trees were left bare, and the little birds stood shivering. They weren't singing their happy tunes anymore.

"Why do you have to cause such misery all the time?" asked the Sun. "It was a beautiful day, and now look what you've done. The birds have nowhere to shelter, and people are rushing into their houses."

But the Wind just laughed. "I like showing how strong I am. You might be happy to just sit around in the sky all day, but I need to use up all my energy and strength."

The Sun looked at the Wind and smiled to herself.

"Why don't we have a contest to see which of us is stronger," said the Sun.

"Ha! It will be a waste of time," cackled the boastful Wind. "You know that I will win!"

"Let's just wait and see," replied the Sun. "See that man down there? Whoever can get him to remove his coat is the strongest. Agreed?"

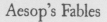

The Wind looked down at the man, who was strolling through a park. Since it was a cold day, he had on a heavy coat to keep him warm.

"Agreed," chuckled the Wind. "This will be easy."

"Go on, then," said the Sun. "I'll hide behind a cloud to keep out of your way."

The Wind, happy to show off again, puffed himself up to his full size and blew and blew. He blew so hard that the fallen leaves swirled around the park, and the poor little birds were nearly blown off the branches as they huddled together for warmth.

The man shivered and pulled up the collar of his coat around his ears.

The Wind blew and blew some more. The birds gave up their struggle and flew off to find somewhere else to shelter. The man pulled up his hood and tightened his scarf around his neck.

The Sun watched from behind the cloud and grinned to herself, as the Wind blew harder and harder and grew more and more furious.

The harder he blew, the tighter the man pulled his coat around his body. The Wind tore angrily at the coat, but all his efforts were in vain.

At last, after one huge and final puff, the Wind called out to the Sun, "My puff is all gone! I need to rest."

The Sun came out from behind the cloud. "All right, I'll take my turn now."

Sulkily, the Wind watched as the Sun began to shine. At first, her rays were gentle. Slowly, the cold air began to warm up. The swirling leaves settled on the ground, and the birds flew back down to perch in the branches of the trees.

The man stopped walking and looked around. It was very pleasant to feel the warmth of the Sun's rays on his face, now that the Wind had stopped blowing.

The Sun shone a little bit brighter. The man loosened his scarf and pulled down his hood.

The Sun breathed in the last of the cold air and sent down more warm rays. The man unbuttoned his coat and let it flap open loosely.

Finally, as the Sun's rays grew warmer and warmer, and she shone more brightly, the man took off his coat and sat down under a tree.

"I think I will take a little rest to enjoy this lovely, unexpected heat," sighed the man happily.

The Wind could not believe his eyes. He huffed angrily in defeat.

"Your freezing blasts of cold air just made the man more determined to keep his coat on, so that he could stay warm," said the Sun wisely. "But my gentle, shining rays made him feel warm, so he no longer needed his coat to protect him from the cold. And look how happy he is now!"

The Wind sighed. He had learned a valuable lesson. Gentleness and kindness are more persuasive than force and bluster.

Moral: Gentle persuasion is better than brute force.

About Aesop's Fables

Aesop's fables started as stories told two thousand years ago. The stories are thought to have been created by a man named Aesop, who was a slave living in Ancient Greece. He watched animals and humans closely and used their characteristics to tell tales and teach lessons: the moral at the end of each story. Short stories with a moral like this are called fables.

Long ago, the stories were passed on by being told aloud. They were used to teach and debate, and they had religious and political themes. Today, the moral lessons are just as useful, and the stories are still told for teaching—as well as for fun!